DEADLY ODDS

Skye sensed the leap of a shadow from his right. Wheeling, he met the attack with a smashing gunbarrel. Two more came at him, catching his gun arm. Bootsteps thudded toward him, and other men landed crushingly atop his shoulders, clubbing him with hardwood truncheons, wrenching his revolver away and battering his skull.

Fargo staggered for footing, bracing his legs wide. He parried a punch with an uppercut and slammed a knee into another attacker's groin. Yet still they swarmed over him like wolves on a hamstrung bull. Twisting, he broke their holds and clubbed them with their own sticks. But it was hopeless.

Then the red haze of pain dimmed—and the Trailsman fell into a blackness as dark as death. . . .

THE TRAILSMAN 71

RENEGADE REBELLION

by
Jon Sharpe

A SIGNET BOOK

NEW AMERICAN LIBRARY

NAL BOOKS ARE AVAILABLE AT QUANTITY DISCOUNTS
WHEN USED TO PROMOTE PRODUCTS OR SERVICES.
FOR INFORMATION PLEASE WRITE TO PREMIUM MARKETING DIVISION,
NEW AMERICAN LIBRARY, 1633 BROADWAY,
NEW YORK, NEW YORK 10019.

Copyright © 1987 by Jon Sharpe

The first chapter of this book previously appeared in
Hostage Arrows, the seventieth volume in this series.

SIGNET TRADEMARK REG. U.S. PAT. OFF. AND FOREIGN COUNTRIES
REGISTERED TRADEMARK—MARCA REGISTRADA
HECHO EN CHICAGO, U.S.A.

SIGNET, SIGNET CLASSIC, MENTOR, ONYX, PLUME, MERIDIAN
AND NAL BOOKS are published by NAL PENGUIN INC.,
1633 Broadway, New York, New York 10019

First Printing, November, 1987

1 2 3 4 5 6 7 8 9

PRINTED IN THE UNITED STATES OF AMERICA

The Trailsman

Beginnings . . . they bend the tree and they mark
the man. Skye Fargo was born when he was eighteen. Terror was his midwife, vengeance his first cry.
Killing spawned Skye Fargo, ruthless, cold-blooded
murder. Out of the acrid smoke of gunpowder still
hanging in the air, he rose, cried out a promise
never forgotten.

The Trailsman, they began to call him, all across
the West: searcher, scout, hunter, the man who
could see where others only looked, his skills for
hire but not his soul, the man who lived each day
to the fullest, yet trailed each tomorrow. Skye Fargo,
the Trailsman, the seeker who could take the wild-
ness of a land and the wanting of a woman and make
them his own.

*Spring, 1859— along the plains and passes
on the death-strewn Overland Trail
where settlers looked ahead to the promised land
—and met disaster.*

1

Forty-four Pittsburgs and Conestogas rolling steadily toward the setting sun. Five hundred mules, half in the traces, half in the *caballada*. One hundred and thirteen farmers and family, lured by the siren call of virgin lands beyond the sunset. And Skye Fargo, the Trailsman, hunter and scout . . .

From Kentucky, the settlers had come by packet up the Missouri River to Independence. Outfitting there, they'd looked for a guide to pilot them on through to California. But it was the end of May, then, the close of the caravan season, and nary a man was to be found. When they checked at the law office, however, the town constable reckoned he knew the whereabouts of one they might hire.

"You could do worse," the constable suggested, fetching a man from a rear jail cell. "Skye Fargo's been to an' fro over every piece of land and every river, since he was whelped."

That the settlers could readily believe. Fargo, fresh from the long trails, stood shaggily unkempt in weathered buckskins and, instead of his usual boots, in parflèche moccasins crafted like none they'd seen before. A Nez Percé squaw had chewed the soles and drawn the sinews for his moccasins in a lodge up in the shadows of the Tetons, a thousand miles away in an uncharted wilderness.

And as they stared askance at the black-whiskered,

fiercely built, roguish frontiersman, the constable told them, "Besides, I'd like to git shut of this brush ape. Less than an hour after hitting town last night, he tore the barbershop apart brawling with five stevadors. Dang near crippled a couple of 'em."

"And I'm going back to skin their hides," Fargo countered, casting the lawman a savage eye. "They'd no call to jump me, using knuckle-dusters and wagon spokes. All I did was dowse some fool in the horse trough when he tried grabbing my turn for a haircut and bath."

"If you won't get while the getting's good, okay, I'll lock you back up. But the gashead you threw in the trough is Colonel Ichabod Remus, who controls most of the wharves in this town, and a pack of men. Remus also happens to be the magistrate who's gonna judge and sentence you, if you're still here."

Fargo stroked his beard. "Well, now, upon second thought . . ."

The train rolled out of Independence with the next dawn, in the teeth of a blustery shower. Spring ran wet and late that year, the frequent rains saturating the midprairies, turning the Overland Trail into a quagmire. When the main trace became too boggy, Fargo would blaze a new off-trail route for firmer traveling, lessening the times they struggled with mud-bogged wheels.

After weeks of wallowing, the train reached the heart of the vast plains beyond the North Platte. For a while now it hadn't rained, and the Rockies—the Shining Mountains the Indians called them—lay like a low bank of blue haze along the far horizon.

They would cross South Pass in three more weeks, Fargo reckoned, barring any delays. It was then he heard a sound from ahead, beyond a low ridge, that stiffened him in his saddle. He sat still on his big Ovaro pinto for a moment longer, listening, and heard it again—the faint crackle of rifle fire. That, he knew, could be only one of two things: either a caravan had come upon a herd of buffalo and was taking meat, or a war party of hostile Indians had come upon a caravan and was taking coup.

Fargo glanced back over his shoulder. The settlers were coming on all right, their wagons strung out over a half-mile of trail behind him, like a great disjointed serpent. Not even Hap Marshall, driving the lead wagon, had heard the sound of gunfire above the rattle of dry fellies and the creak of linchpins.

There was no use in alarming them, Fargo knew, until he discovered the cause of the shooting. He doffed his wide-brimmed hat from his jet-black hair. It was enough for now to let Marshall, the wagon boss, know he was going to check on something that lay beyond the next ridge, and Marshall answered with a wave, nodding as Fargo pointed ahead.

Fargo put his black-and-white Ovaro into a run. Stopping below the ridge line, he drop-reined his mount and covered the last distance on foot until, crouching in the tall prairie grass so his figure would not be silhouetted, he peered across the ridge. Green-gray, the prairie stretched away on all sides. Whipped by the afternoon breeze, the grass waved across the swells of the plain, like the incessant rolling of the Pacific that lay beyond the Rockies and Sierras. There was a vast grandeur in the scene, but Fargo paid it little heed. Instead, his lake-blue eyes chilled as he viewed the nightmare of all westbound immigrants.

A half-mile ahead in the bottom of the next prairie swale stood a Conestoga, its canvas billowing in the breeze. Twin puffs of smoke came from behind one front wheel. As he stared at the puffs, he realized only two rifles were down there, only two to stave off the attack of fifty Dakota warriors. Whoever they were, they hadn't a chance if they didn't get help fast. Even as he watched, a war chief signaled with his white battle shield, and Fargo saw the circle of hard-riding warriors tighten about the doomed wagon. A cloud of arrows sped from their short bows.

Fargo squirmed back out of sight, and at a run, reached his Ovaro. Low in the saddle, he started his race against time, and as he rode a pair of questions pestered him. How, he asked himself, had that wagon ever got separated from its caravan? What kind of captain would leave one lone Conestoga behind on this death-infested strip between the Platte and the Rockies?

He drew to a sharp halt alongside Marshall's wagon.

"What's up?" Marshall yelled. He was a diminutive man, in boots, clothes, and hat that appeared too big for him. White hair curled about his ears, and luxuriant burnsides bushed out from his leathery cheeks. He looked like a sharp-faced terrier and he had all of a terrier's scrappy courage.

"Fifty Dakotas have a wagon surrounded up ahead," Fargo called. "Get your horse and bring your rifle!"

At each wagon, Fargo repeated his call to arms, and men he'd been schooling for just such an emergency as this wasted no time. In minutes they were all gathered at Marshall's wagon, features implacable. This was still-contested Indian territory, and fellowman helped fellowman here. Death might be waiting for some of them up ahead, and yet none showed their fear. The only trouble was that some of these brave Kentuckians might be too brave, brave to the point of recklessness.

"What's holding us up?" Hap Marshall demanded in his caustic voice. "There's thirty of us, and that ought to be enough to roll those damn Dakotas back to the Rockies."

Fargo smiled mirthlessly. Marshall's bragging reinforced his suspicion of a moment before. "We're hold-

12

ing up because you men have to know what you're up against," he said evenly. "A Dakota can plant three arrows in a circle the size of your hat while you're loading one ball. They know that, and we'll pay in blood if we try to rush them."

"We ain't gonna let them folks get scalped, blood or no blood!" the young, hot-tempered Abel Rasmussen argued.

Fargo shook his head at the impetuous homesteader. "Not if we can help it," he agreed, "but neither do we want any widows crying themselves to sleep tonight. So, I've mapped out a plan. When we get to the ridge, half of us will go over. Hap, you string out the right, and ride single-file just close enough to the tip so those Dakotas can see your heads. Ride like hell for a hundred yards, then circle back out of sight and do it over again. I'll be missing the mark if that doesn't make those braves think we've got a big party held in reserve."

Hap Marshall's rheumy eyes sparkled as he studied Fargo. "Son, you've learned a thing or two crossin' these plains before," he exclaimed. "C'mon, you Kentucky clodhoppers, we'll make them redskins think a whole army is waiting to ride 'em down if they don't skedaddle!"

With a final yell of "Just remember to hold your fire till we get within range! Empty guns won't stop arrows," Fargo led the way at a gallop. In his saddle boot was his Sharps rifle, while snugged at his thigh was one of Samuel Colt's percussion revolvers, which he now drew as they charged down across the ridge.

Down below, the Dakotas were busy hurling arrows at the harried defenders. Their whoops of triumph changed to howls of shock as a salvo of gunfire burst from the slope. Three Dakotas crumpled. The survivors whirled, dazed with alarm, ducking and dodging as lead stormed around them.

Some tried to rally, firing wildly at the onrushing men, volleys of arrows spearing through the air. Fargo heard them hiss close by like aroused snakes. Riding near enough to see the paint that glowed on high-cheeked faces, he fired again, and again, turning hawk-beaked visages red with blood. An arrow bedded itself with a sodden thud into the high cantle of his saddle.

The immigrant fighters, yelling and swearing, stormed on with careless abandon, the plain reverberating with the blasts of their weapons. The most stubborn of Dakotas began to break now, turning their frantic horses and seeking cover. Two more bit the dust, another choked with pain as a bullet smashed his arm. But the Indians didn't panic. Disciplined, they speedily fanned out and around, bringing their bows into play to cover their retreat. A broad swath of arrows rained down into the settlers as they reached the wagon, forcing them to rein in and slew aside to avoid the shafts.

But it was only a temporary delay, the settlers spurring on even as the arrows clattered about the prairie. The Dakotas scattered every which way across the plain. Only a rough dozen out of the original pack remained in striking distance, although the tall grass and their constant movement made it difficult to count them. In their midst rode the chieftain, white shield and pennoned lance held high.

Fargo was determined to down the leader, if at all possible. He halted as the other men chased after the braves, and quickly shouldered his Sharps, took a careful bead, and squeezed the trigger. He caught the man nearest the leader, as the chief zigged and the other man zagged at the last possible instant. The man toppled against the other's black horse, which shied and almost unseated its rider, who hurriedly urged the animal out of Fargo's gunsights. Before he could rechamber and gain his bead again, the Dakotas had fled like wraiths into the protective screen of grass and gullies.

The settlers were reining in about the Trailsman's Ovaro now. One husky Kentucky farmer looked a little pale about the lips, and grinned shakily. "We were sure teaching them a lesson," he said in a nasal drawl, "and I for one, am glad to be endin' it now. Fightin' nature behind a plow is one thing; fightin' men that're ready to kill you is somethin' else! I just hope we got here in time to save them folks in that wagon."

"We done that, all right," another settler muttered. "I can see someone crawlin' out from behind that front wheel."

Fargo looked toward the Conestoga, and his brows raised with involuntary surprise. Two women in billowing skirts were beside the wagon now, one of them waving her sunbonnet at them.

"Glory be," he heard Lem Clarke sigh. "Two petticoats! I hope they ain't good-lookers. If they be, my ol' woman won't let me out of her sight between here and California!"

Fargo smiled at Clarke's comments, but his lips were straight again when they drew near the battered prairie schooner, for his eyes had already picked out the bulky shape of a dead man lying in the shadow cast by the wagon's high tilt. Fargo felt his ire rise again: the immigrant's death had been unnecessary. This Conestoga should never have been deserted here. But there'd be time enough to talk of that later. Right now these women needed what comfort they could give them.

The elder of the pair was crouched over the dead man, tugging vainly at the arrows pincushioning his body. She raised a tear-washed face to Fargo as he reined to a halt alongside her.

"Ma'am . . ." Fargo held his hat in his big hands. "Ma'am, you better let some of us tackle that chore."

It was the younger woman who answered Fargo as he dismounted. Her voice was dull, rough-edged from the gunpowder fumes. "You're very kind," she said. "I . . . I guess Father wouldn't have felt so bad about dying if he'd known help was coming."

Fargo looked at the girl, and his first impression was of enormous eyes in an elfin face. Eyes that were as dark as the black powder smudges on her white cheeks. He noted that horror had given the girl's lips a bitter, down-curving twist, and he realized, with curiosity, that it had taken more than this battle and loss of her father to put it there.

Bronze-hued hair that long since had lost its sheen straggled across the girl's forehead. She reached up now with a woman's instinctive gesture to rearrange it, and Fargo noted that her arm was little more than skin and bone. Her body, too, beneath its shapeless brown calico, seemed flat. And yet Fargo had the feeling that she had not always looked this way. Once the immigrant girl had worn nice clothes and her face and figure had been lovely as any. She was another casualty of the trace—the Overland Trail had robbed her of beauty, and now of her father.

The girl was studying Skye Fargo as intently, and she was seeing in the husky six-footer a strength many men lacked. He was full-bearded, and the dust of travel had caked thickly along the lean cut of his cheekbones and about his firm lips. It was his eyes, though, set wide on either side of a big aquiline nose, that attracted her most. The blue of them mirrored hurts and scars, tragedies she could not fathom, giving her a sense of kinship with her own sorrow. The brazenness of her scrutiny brought a little color to her cheeks. She held out her hand, and Fargo took it gravely.

"My name is Julia Talbot," the girl said, "and this is my mother, Elaine. I—we don't know just how to thank you, Mister—"

"Fargo. Call me Skye." He turned to the bunched settlers who had not dismounted, ordering, "You men ride back and bring up the wagons. If I remember right, there ought to be a stand of hardwoods and a spring across the next rise. We'll circle there for the night. Meantime I'll stay with these people and see what shape their wagon is in."

As the men rode off, Elaine Talbot looked up from where she still crouched beside her husband. "Oh, the wagon will roll," she said in a low, bitter tone. "My Sam got it fixed just before those Indians found us here. But it took two days, and Olin Karnes wouldn't wait."

Fargo understood what had detained them as his roving glance took in a pile of hickory shavings and the broken spindle of an axle. Such accidents were common on a long trek, and laying over while new axles were fashioned or spare ones installed was an accepted part of overland travel. His rising hackles harshened his voice.

"You mean this Karnes wouldn't hold up while you fixed that axle?"

Mrs. Talbot nodded. She too had once been beautiful, but now there was heartbreak in her face and voice. "We're from St. Louis," she began. "Sam had a good mercantile business there, but so many folks talked to him about how much money the storekeepers were making out West that he just up and sold the business right out from under us. He loaded this wagon, bundled me and Julia into it, and traipsed to Independence. Sam was no plainsman, but when we reached Council Grove, he managed to hook up with Olin Karnes."

"They only had ten wagons," her daughter said, seeming anxious to take up the story, "but there were five men for each of them. That made a party of fifty. I didn't care for them much, but Dad said they were

Missourians like us, and Missouri folk were the salt of the earth."

"We found out different soon enough," Mrs. Talbot said dismally. "Only it was too late then to turn back. Julia didn't have a minute . . ."

"Go on," Fargo urged tersely.

Mrs. Talbot shrugged. "When the axle broke, Olin Karnes gave Sam his choice. He'd hold up the train till it was fixed, if Julia would . . . would go stay with him, openly. Otherwise they'd go on without us."

It was easy to see the family's choice. Sam Talbot had valued honor more than life. Looking from the dead man to the women, Fargo said slowly, "The devil reserves a particular corner in hell for men like Olin Karnes."

Later, as evening shadows softened the outlines of the plain, Fargo stood with bared head at the foot of Sam Talbot's grave. All the wagon-train folk were gathered about the mound of earth with him, as Marshall intoned a simple verse from the black prayer book in his hand. When Marshall was through, Fargo sensed that the company was waiting for him to add some final word. He was no speaker, avoided such palaver whenever possible, but managed to get through it when called upon.

"Death is something we all have to face on a trip like this," he said quietly. "Right now it looks like Sam Talbot died for nothing, but in the big scheme of things maybe there's a reason for his going. There're always some brave ones who have to take that chance or the world wouldn't advance much. You folks are going to a new land. It means promise for some, suffering for others. I'm hoping you Talbots will find a new life in California. I'm hoping everyone in the train will. And let's remember that looking backward never solved any problems. We're going on, we're going ahead. Hang and rattle, and we'll come out on top."

Julia Talbot found her way to Fargo's campfire later that same evening.

Hap Marshall was there as well, chewing the rag and sharing a bit of corn liquor. He saw her first and scrambled awkwardly to his feet. "Gotta get a fresh pail o' water," he declared. "Yep, we're all out." Then he proved himself a liar by stumbling over the camp bucket and spilling its full contents across the hard-packed ground.

Fargo stretched with the lazy, tawny grace of a mountain cougar and rose to meet the approaching girl. He grinned at Marshall. "Guess we do need some water at that."

Julia's gaunt cheeks looked pink to Fargo as she halted directly in front of him. "I only wanted to thank you again for the wonderful things you're doing for me and Mother," she said softly.

Fargo took her hands. "You don't need to thank me for a thing, Julia. Save such talk until after I meet up with Olin Karnes."

Returning from the spring, Hap Marshall heard those grave words, and to him they seemed to ring with a note of prophecy.

2

Other prophetic words had been spoken that night as the Kentucky farmsteaders were to remember. Skye Fargo had told them to look ahead, to hang and rattle. In the following days that bunched into weeks, "hang and rattle" became a slogan.

The shouted phrase helped toiling men drive creaking wagons across the backbone of the continent. It was a laboriously hard trek, especially when fording the swollen runoffs streaming dangerously from upland storms. Worry, exhaustion, frustration, grueling vigilance, ever-threatened injury and illness—these were factors as menacing as breakdowns or Indians.

It tested Hap Marshall's leadership more than anything since the company had elected him wagon master in Kentucky. Fargo had no truck with camp gossip and feuds, and often was away scouting or hunting game for the kettles, but he backed the greenhorn boss, taking over the duty of prescribing routes and stops. Other than that, Marshall ruled the roost, brash and iron-willed, impatient of delay. His chief weapon was his tongue, which he didn't let rust, badgering some, shaming others, and bringing quarrelsome scrappers in line with cutting scorn.

In addition to the expected perils, Fargo started noticing the rise of another, man-made hazard.

At first he sensed a tension, like a brewing undercurrent. It began soon after the Talbots joined, while he was still keeping a wary eye on their wagon for any signs of difficulties. But that wasn't the problem; Elaine Talbot kept pace and managed her outfit with sturdy competence. Neighborly and circumspect, she won over the train wives and caught glances of the husbands as lessening grief and regular meals filled out her gauntness. Elaine was recovering to her old self, a prime-looking woman, Fargo noted, and he suspected she'd also been the bulwark of the Talbot family. She combined stamina and pluck, what in a horse would be prized as "bottom," though Fargo wasn't too sure Elaine would thrill to hear that compliment.

Her daughter Julia also had bottom, which she twitched most fetchingly. And it fetched in the fellows, too. She was an outrageous flirt to all, granting special favors to none, except perhaps on Thursdays, as Fargo had cause to remember and, at moments, regret.

Badly smitten, Abel Rasmussen pursued Julia pawing and snorting like a spavined bull ox. He and his father had left their Kentucky home following the death of his mother, and now while Abel chased love, Oscar Rasmussen sought whiskey, drinking on their wagon all day and at their cook fire all night. Abel was touchy about his father, and had an even pricklier jealous streak when it came to Julia. He wasn't mean-spirited, merely a quick-tempered, quick-fisted stud over six feet tall and two hundred pounds, who could plant most anybody with one poke.

He was a powerful temptation for a tease like Julia. She must have said something to Abel, for increasingly he lurked and loomed around Fargo, eyes glaring, lips working, hand on the knife at his belt. It was equally evident to Fargo that Julia had not told all, for Abel had yet to call him out. They'd have surely locked horns by now, if jealous, resentful Abel had known about that very first night after the Talbots were rescued.

It had been during the dark early hours, that night, when Fargo awoke needing to go take a leak. The cook fires had died down and the enclosure of circled wagons was a resonant black pocket of grumblings and snores. He arose quietly, making his way over the chains fastening the wheels of the two nearest wagons, and headed across a short stretch of open field toward a nearby clump of trees.

A guard reared out of the grass, gun barrel gleaming faintly.

"It's okay," Fargo murmured. "Sit down, Cousins."

Emery Cousins, a short, balding settler, nodded and disappeared.

Fargo continued on, into the concealing brush of the copse. Pissing, he heard a faint scratching noise from beyond the brush, and when it ceased a moment later, he chalked it up to a foraging rodent. He started back out . . .

And collided with Julia as she rushed from around the brushy fringe. He almost brained her before recognizing who it was.

"Don't hit! It's me!" She cuddled against him, like a cat seeking affection, her voice faltering. "Oh, I'm glad it's you. I feel so alone, Mr. Fargo . . . Skye. I've been lying, tossing and turning, sick, just sick about all this. And if I do fall asleep a little, I dream awful nightmares that scare me awake." Her chin trembled, a portent of tears. "You must think me such a child."

"No, and don't you think it. Everyone lets their hair down now and then, and after all you've suffered, nobody deserves to more than you."

"It's you who deserve everything," she murmured, scrutinizing him with misty eyes, her uptilted face yearning. "You saved our lives today, and I'm very grateful. Very grateful."

Fargo was growing interested, but he was also growing worried about playing her game. He wondered how far she'd tease, how far was too far, and he didn't care to face any uproar tonight. "Julia, you've already thanked me—"

"I know." She laid her hands on his chest, palms flat, fingers kneading. "I want to thank you again, in a more private way." She pressed her body against him, her arm circling his back and clinging as she kissed him for a long, burning moment. Fargo responded with enthusiasm, returning her kiss, feeling her lips clinging hungrily, her breasts mashing against his chest, her hands along his hips.

Julia broke their embrace, then, as abruptly as she'd clung, and eyed Fargo with a kind of frenzy. "We can't stay here."

Fargo nodded. Cousins or anyone coming from the wagons to relieve themselves might see them. Everyone would, knowing his luck. And if they were seen, he had a hunch it would cause one hell of a stink hereabouts.

"Come with me."

"But—"

"Come with me," she insisted, her tone brooking no argument. Julia was barefoot, and she was quick on her toes in more ways than one. Pulling Fargo by the hand, she darted back deeper into the grove, threading through a tangle of rocks, brush, and trees until they reached a mound of boulders. As they moved through the screening rock, Fargo noticed it encircled a small clearing of bucknut, sage, and foot-high tufts of bluegrass.

Julia then showed him a different nature lesson, backing him up against one of the boulders, squeezing so close to him that he could feel her hotly beating pulse. They began kissing again, and as often as Fargo kissed her, Julia paid back the kiss with wanton interest. Until finally she drew away and stood in front of him, provocatively undressing, exposing smooth, unblemished skin, pointed breasts topped by raspberry-sized nipples, and a plump pudenda with lips accentuated by a thin line of velvety curls.

Aroused, Fargo hastened out of his clothes. Julia stretched out on the grass, watching him strip with a vacant, burnt expression. She was breathing hard, as though there wasn't enough air in the clearing when, naked, Fargo lay alongside and embraced her. His hands moved compulsively, spreading tenderly across her flat stomach and up over her perky breasts. Trembling from his touch, she shuddered and gripped him, pulling him, urging his hand to slide between her legs and along her sleek inner thighs. Her hips slackened, widening to allow him access while she kept murmuring in a low, passionate voice, "Take me, take me, fill me . . ."

But Fargo was not quite ready to take her, licking the curve of her neck first and then lower, nuzzling and kissing one breast at a time. His groin pressed against her pubic bone, and he began pumping his jutting erection along the sensitive crevice between her thighs, never quite penetrating her.

Julia opened and closed her eyes, gasping and whimpering. Her buttocks jerked and quivered, her legs rolling and squirming until they were splayed out on the grass. "Don't tease me, Skye," she mewled, panting harshly. "Put it in, oh, please put it in." In a frenzy, she reached between them and placed his taunting member against the opening of her moist sheath, prodding Fargo into herself with her own trembling fingers.

"Now," she sighed breathlessly, seeming to swallow

the whole of him up inside her small belly as she arched her back. "Now . . ."

Crooning, Julia kicked her feet out and locked clawing arms and legs firmly around Fargo's impaling body. He felt her eager young muscles tightening smoothly around him in a pressuring action of their own, and he set his mind to the delicious ecstasy of the moment. Tighter she wrapped her limbs, deeper she sank her fingernails, rhythmically matching Fargo's building tempo as his body pounded hers against the matting bluegrass.

A rain-softened grassy patch is not the ideal spot, Fargo thought dizzily, for such frantic sport. But that was about all he thought as they panted in concentration, Julia pushing her pelvis upward in an arc to devour his hardened flesh pistoning into her belly. Faint cries of animal pleasure rose from her throat, her face contorting with desire, her thighs rhythmically squeezing as Fargo quickened his thrusts, searing and pulsating.

"Ohhhh . . ." she cried, the exquisite agony of impending orgasm making her writhe beneath him. "Come with me," she pleaded loudly as Fargo felt her inner sheath contracting spasmodically from her erupting orgasm. Fargo climaxed with her, spurting deep inside her milking belly. And long after they were both good for nothing, Julia was still wailing, "Come with me, come!"

"I have, I have," Fargo groaned, settling down over her soft warm body. He lay, crushing her breasts and belly with his weight, while his immediate satiation began to wane.

"God, you feel so good," Julia sighed, hugging him affectionately and claiming the last drops of joy there between her legs. "I tell you, Skye, I tell you true. If I don't get my itch scratched every Thursday, I simply fall to pieces. And I missed last week."

"Thursday? Y'mean, you got this scheduled?"

"Why, we do everything else in life by the calendar or clock. Sex should be orderly and in its proper place, too, not haphazard like dumb animals."

He rolled from her then, unwilling to argue, and began to gently stroke her breasts.

She smiled at him. "You'll get me going again."

"Great, but not now. We should be getting back."

"Later," she replied lazily. But within a minute she was on her feet, yawning and stretching as Fargo grabbed for his pants. "I suppose we must get a move on," she pouted, looking disappointed as she retrieved her clothes. She was still smoothing them out as they started back to the wagons, appearing fresh and dangerously eager for more.

Shortly, as they came out of the copse by the edge of the field, Fargo said, "It looks like nothing's happened, nobody's the wiser. Let's keep it that way. You go first, and I'll go in fifteen, twenty minutes."

Julia slowed, her hips rubbing his thighs. "If you hear me scream, you'll know Momma got wiser and not to come in." She rose on tiptoe and her breath was a hiss in his ear, "Momma's such a prude. She'd kill me, and you, if she ever found out." Then giving Fargo a peck on his cheek, she hurried to the wagons and vanished inside their corral.

Fargo began pacing off the time, half-expecting to hear her scream. Sooner or later, he was sure, that female would get some fool buck killed while trying to fill her Thursday appointment. He just hoped that once he got back into his bedroll, that'd mark the end and nothing further would come of it.

Nothing had, so far. In that sense, Fargo felt it safe to assume Julia hadn't laid bare her past, as a switch, but was only raising cain with a blooming idiot, Abel. But unquestionably the mischievous minx presented a hazard, a very man-made hazard. The unpredictable sort, ticklish and delicate to handle, potentially damaging, even explosive, if ever exposed suddenly without warning, or in the wrong light.

As the settlers wheeled their wagons over high South Pass, into the headwaters of streams whose destination was the Pacific Ocean, the hazard came close to cutting loose.

The next day they rolled on down the Rockies to Green River. Come night, they made camp in the Green River bottoms, a quarter-mile from a roaring torrent that made talk difficult. Fires were blazing when Skye Fargo rode into the circle, a blacktail on his pack, trouble on his mind. "Looked at the river," he informed Hap Marshall. "Don't like it."

"I'll have God change it for you," Marshall gibed mockingly. "What's your grouch?"

"It's no hoorah, Hap. The Green's boiling bank-full carrying plenty of big snags. It'll be a hell of a stream to ford."

"You claiming we can't? Hell, we gotta cross."

Fargo shrugged. "Risky, but not impossible. The bank is shallow sloping at one point, a good spot to launch from. We could caulk the boxes, buoy them with trees, and try ferrying the wagons across there behind swimming teams."

"Ain't no trying, we're doing. We're going where we're going," Marshall declared with a curling lip. "Tell you what, you crawfish. You like to gamble. I'll lay you two to one that you'll have us camped on the west bank tomorrow night. Put up or shut up!"

Fargo grinned and shut up. That was Hap. Even while chafing from his rawhiding, Fargo had to admire his bodacious spunk.

Daylight was filtering into the bottomlands when Hap Marshall's "Hang 'n' rattle!" caused men to drain their coffeecups and rush for their animals. Dozens of fires flickered against the circled tilts, dispelling the damp chill.

Fargo went for his picketed horse, and was placing the saddle when his name was called. "Skye!" Turning, he saw Julia Talbot come out of the brushy shadows, approaching with a nervous impatience, looking beguilingly chaste and vulnerable in a blue gingham frock and sunbonnet. She stopped close in front of him, tense and anxious. Fargo made no gesture to comfort Julia, no arm about her or pat on the shoulder, as he asked what was bothering her.

"The Green, it—it's dangerous, Skye. Must we cross now?"

"Waiting till it gets better might stall us for weeks," he replied quietly. "Every day counts, if we're to reach California ahead of the Sierra winter."

"I don't care, I'm frightened by the river, terribly. Momma's dreadfully afraid of losing control and foundering, but . . . Well, Abel offered to serve as our driver." She smiled ruefully, glancing up with her dark, entreating eyes. "We haven't the heart to refuse him, you understand. But when we cross, Skye, would you watch after us?"

"I will, Julia. Go assure your mother. I'll stay on the lookout, and Abel'll escort you fine. These wagons aren't called prairie boats for nothing."

She swayed against him. "You're a dear. I think of you, Thursdays."

"Well, today's not Thursday," Fargo said, growing chary of her coy intimations. "Quit worrying. Get along now." He nudged her away and stood watching her hasten toward the wagons. "Jesus Christ, what a little minx," he murmured wondrously.

Fargo turned to his cinch, hitched the latigo, dropped the stirrup leather. As he mounted, a young man emerged from the timber, riding one mule, leading five others. Powerfully built, with calloused hands and thick legs, his neck reared alarmingly from sloping shoulders, with his broad features crowned by an unruly thatch of chestnut hair. His eyes were narrowed suspiciously as he began, "Listen here, Fargo, I—"

"Stalking wide again, eh, Rasmussen?" Fargo cut in. "You forgetting Hap Marshall's orders?"

"Never mind me, Fargo," Abel Rasmussen said sullenly. "I laid out last night." He patted his big revolver. "If Indians ever rush my mules, I'll get some scalps." His eyes flicked toward the confusion at the wagons. "Julia just left you, didn't she?"

"Sure. Why?"

Rasmussen's lips flattened. "She's my gal. You steer clear."

Fargo grinned coldly. "And if I don't?"

"Damn my soul, mister, I'll kill you dead." He started his mules as Marshall's voice rang, "All set? All set? Get them teams spanned, be quick about it!"

Fargo rode thoughtfully after the mules, knowing Abel Rasmussen meant it. He would slay to keep another from his woman. A sense of inescapable trouble touched Fargo. Since that first night, he had made no effort to fiddle around with Julia. Now he would make less effort to avoid her. If Abel Rasmussen was spoiling to fight, the sooner they had it out, the better. Then it'd all be over and done with.

Ha.

His troubles were just beginning.

3

Skye Fargo and Hap Marshall sat on their horses at the bank of the torrent that surged, high and swift, toward the far, deep canyons of the Colorado and the distant Gulf of California. Driftwood and uprooted bushes swept past, bucking and weaving, careening off rocks and plummeting on. Here and there oily, long whorls of deep-brown mud churned to the roiling surface, sucking flotsam under.

Crowding around them and along the shoreline, the settlers stared at the river in dismay and trepidation. Every man, woman, and child was scared. Maybe Hap was scared, too, but if he was, no hint of it showed on his dogged face.

"Is this the creek that scared you?" he scoffed. "Hell, I've crossed worse without gettin' my boots wet."

Fargo nodded. "Yes, by spanning it hip-deep in your bullshit."

"Damn your eyes," Marshall chortled. "I just may, if you don't know anything about river-hopping, except how to jump steamboat floozies. C'mon, start moving! We're burning daylight!"

Fargo wheeled his Ovaro, lifted his hand, and his voice sheered through the bawdy voice of the river, rolling back along the wagons. "Out with the axes. Form cutting squads of four. Pick out tall trees—two twenty-footers and two twelve-footers to each wagon.

Don't let grass grow under your boots; we have a long haul ahead."

Men muttered, prophesying disaster, but they obeyed. Soon the axes rang through the timber, and tall, gnarled cottonwoods crashed and were stripped of tops and branches. Ready hands lifted the logs and bore them to the wagons, where Fargo directed them to be lashed with ropes to the beds, butt ends forward over the doubletrees, the shorter boles lashed across them, fore and aft. Others, meanwhile, calked the wagon beds as watertight as possible, packing the seams and cracks with oakum, pine tar, and any handy filler.

The sun crawled up across the sky. Men sweated and cursed and chopped. It was near midafternoon when the last makeshift raft was roped in place and Marshall took over from Fargo, giving the order to roll. No man wanted to be first, no man but bleary Oscar Rasmussen, reining alone on his wagon while son Abel drove the Talbot's. Dejected and resentful, Oscar was full of bravado, too well stewed in corn liquor to fear for himself.

"Rabbits, that's what they are," he proclaimed. "Scared of their shadows. I'll show 'em. Just me myself will lead your damn train across. Follow me!" Oscar pulled out of line, his long blacksnake curling over his team as he lashed them into a run toward the river.

"Put up that whip, you rummy hooch-hound!" Marshall bellowed. "Give those mules their heads, just enough rein to keep 'em pointed upstream!"

Oscar gave a whoop, set the whip in its sock, and let the mules tear ahead of their bulky, swaying load. They hit the water with a fountaining splash. The leaders buckled to their knees, and were instantly rolled on their sides. The span behind plunged past and were rolled down upon their teammates. For a moment, the outfit seemed hopelessly tangled. Then an eddy carried the leaders down and the six animals fell into line, swimming diagonally downstream.

Fargo, yelling orders lost in the tumult of the waters, launched into a gallop. Oscar Rasmussen cast a sidelong glance at Fargo as he passed and, seeming to grasp the import of the commands, began sawing the lines. He was suddenly cold-sober and his vein-netted face was gray with fear. Fargo plunged his Ovaro into the rushing flow, raising a great shower of spray, and prodded his horse toward Rasmussen's lead mules. At that moment, the wagon was almost swamped by a floating tree, its spidery base of severed roots flailing the muddy surface like desperate arms.

It was a chilling thing to watch, a thing that could easily leach out the last of the settlers' courage, effectively deterring them from the challenge. Fargo cast a swift glance at the bank, and was gratified to see that Hap Marshall had also realized the threat. Marshall was reining his teams out of the line and spanked them into a run, waving the others on. He hit the water headed sharply upstream, and he held them thus as his leaders began swimming without mishap.

Downstream, Fargo was having trouble overtaking Rasmussen. The current dragged at the legs of the Ovaro, swirling and splashing against the saddle skirts. The roots of the snag had somehow locked in Rasmussen's wagon wheels, and the whole rigmarole floated with the current, the top of the tree slewing erratically.

Oscar Rasmussen, utterly panic-stricken, had relaxed his rein pressure, drawn his whip, and was lashing the near leader. Fargo could see Hap Marshall's gnarled face livid with rage, even at this distance, as he ventured another glance behind him. The line of wagons was trundling riverward, taking the water each in his turn. The die was cast now.

The Rasmussen outfit continued downstream at an alarming rate. The shiftings of the tree caused the wagon to reel and pitch in dizzying lurches, knocking Rasmussen constantly off-kilter. A crushing swell seemed to engulf the wagon like a tidal wave. Staggering, legs wobbling, Oscar Rasmussen careened against the low side of the seat box and, with a roupy squawk, tumbled over the edge. The wagon bobbed upright, buoyed by its raft, jouncing and wallowing, but Fargo could see no sign of Rasmussen.

With fading hope he might spot the drunk, Fargo tried to keep an eye on the downriver side of the wagon. But the closer he came, the worse the angle, until finally he gave up and got his Ovaro turned to the rig—a risky maneuver—quit his saddle, and caught the seat rail. The horse floundered for a moment, quickly recovered, and began swimming for the west bank as the river swept him and the wagon on.

Hoisting himself into the wagon box, Fargo nearly joined his horse and Rasmussen in the dunk, stumbling over a whiskey bottle rolling loose on the box floor. Wavering, groping for support, he caught his balance and scanned the downstream surface—no Rasmussen—then glanced directly below at the enmeshed tree and saw the man sprawled on the bole where he'd fallen, sticking to his gnarly perch with a frantic stranglehold on the roots.

"Hang on!" Fargo called down to him. "We'll try to make shore. Work your way up. If the tree breaks loose, swim for the west bank, okay?"

Rasmussen nodded yes repeatedly, his eyes closed, his lips moving as if he prayed.

Fargo straightened, chucked the bottle into the wagon bed, muttering, "The luck of drunks," then wrenched a commanding pressure on the reins that drew the leaders about.

But other driftwood kept piling on, in turn catching more flotsam, forming a floating dam that increased Fargo's downstream momentum. He tried desperately to get a burst of effort from the swimming teams, to at least clear the debris from around them, but they slammed broadside into an uprooted saltbush of massive girth. There was a wrenching crash of breaking limbs, and a wave broke over the wagon, drenching Fargo. Even as it subsided and he was feeling relieved to spot Rasmussen still clinging tenaciously below, Fargo heard a faint cry from under the canvas.

His blood ran cold as he heard it again. Somebody was back in the wagon, trapped among the Rasmussen goods and farm implements, caught in the rush of water over the sideboards.

The mules were struggling to thrash free, and Fargo could do nothing to help them. He knew the risk of abandoning the reins, but whoever that was must have help. A caulked wagon bed would hold water, which could easily drown a body trapped in it. Hitching the reins by the rail, Fargo vaulted the seat and forged rearward through the load, searching hurriedly, yelling, "Who called?"

No answer. Shoving on, he found crates and casks, seed bags of corn and wheat, a dismantled plow and harrow, the whiskey bottle again, and two feet of water in the wagon bed; but he found no sign of life. "I heard you," he snapped testily, wading by the plow, "C'mon, where are—"

His boot struck something yielding. Reaching down, he caught his fingers in hair and pulled a head to the surface. The head, he discerned, of a youth. The lad was half-conscious, gagging, woozily stirring. And he was caught between a barrel and a packing case. Nor could Fargo extricate him until, by brute force, he jerked the barrel back and fished the kid out of the water.

He was a redheaded ragamuffin in patched dungarees and sodden boots, and a scruffy black hat dangling by its whang cord. At his belt hung a bone-handled knife and an old Adams .44 pistol, each encased in a soft home-made holster. His shirt was a linsey-woolsey pullover many sizes too large for him, with a ragged gash and a spreading bloodstain up on the left side. On his left temple was a livid bruise, raw and pulpy. He'd fallen hard, okay, but he was rising tough, choking, gasping, weak but gamely struggling. "Lemme go!"

Fargo ignored his protests, noting his bruise while drawing him up to where the light was better. Saying, "Hell of a goose egg," Fargo began pulling up the boy's shirt. "It's not broken or bleeding . . . Hold still!"

Contrarily the boy grew more unruly, making an intense effort to twist away while clutching his shirt closed.

"Kid, you got cut, you don't know how bad or what you fell on," Fargo argued, seizing his wrists. "Like the dirty rusted plow blade right there."

The boy kept squirming and jerking fitfully, teeth bared in a grimace. "Leggo! Leave me alone!"

Forcing his arms together, Fargo snapped, "You're bleeding like a stuck pig, and I haven't time to fart around," as he got hold of both wrists in one hand, leaving his other hand free. He yanked the shirt upward.

Buckled around the boy's lean waist was a money belt, its glove-leather pouches closed and bulging fat. Well, that explained the little bastard's tent-sized shirt and scrappy resistance, Fargo thought, hitching the shirt higher toward the wound . . . and revealing a pair of taut, perky breasts like succulent white apples, with rosy-pink nipples springing firm from their tips.

For a blink of an eye, Fargo was taken aback, his eyes stared in wonder. The girl's continuing struggles stirred her breasts to swing and bobble, making it difficult to size up her wound. It was a slashing gouge along her left breast, appearing at first glimpse to be shallow and clean, the sort of flesh wound that bleeds profusely without real injury . . . if tended to. Well, she deserved tending, he thought, considering her tenacity, her ardor, her spirit, her pert breasts swaying . . .

Her head darted down, her sharp teeth sinking into his wrist. Pain and surprise made Fargo release her. Next instant she had unsheathed her bone-handled knife and was darting close, its wicked skinning blade lancing directly for his gizzard. Reflexively he swung his arm, blocking her thrust and deflecting her arm aside. He almost managed to bat the knife out of her grip, but she recovered and immediately stabbed again.

This time he caught her knife wrist on an out-flung hand. He was about to apply the pressure to disarm her when the wagon jolted abruptly. His hold broke, and the girl was torn free, knife skittering off somewhere in the load. She struck the packing case and clung to keep from falling.

Fargo was knocked staggering into the water sloshing around the plow. The mules must have broken loose from the debris, he realized, but the wagon must have stayed snagged; he could hear the sound made by the running gear scraping against the tree. So Rasmussen was still riding along; the souse was sticking to that tree, tighter now than he'd ever been tight in his life before. Or so Fargo reckoned as he went swooping after the whiskey bottle that he'd tossed rearward. He found it at once, right where he recalled, and immediately dived the few paces back to the girl.

"You won't die from embarrassing, but you can from festering." He handed her the bottle and also his kerchief, wary of surprise moves. But the girl merely regarded him quizzically as she took them, standing inimically, panting through clenched teeth. "Okay, you got alcohol to wash in, not drink, and a compress or whatever." Fargo would have stayed as instructor, except that the wagon was moving across again and he could spare no time. Turning to go, he added, "And step lively. Get your clothes on, soon as you can."

"Why? Does it bother you?" she taunted.

"Not if it doesn't bother you," he replied, glancing back with a wry grin. "But you're liable to bother quite a lot of people on this train."

For the barest fraction of a moment the girl's eyes looked squarely at him. Many redheads have greenish eyes, but her's were eyes of true emerald, turbulently iridescent. And it seemed to Fargo that he read a desperate message in their troubled depths, a plea for help. Then he scrambled over the load, leapt into the box, and saw that the team had indeed broken free of debris. And as luck would shine, they wound up more or less pointed right, and he set to pressuring the noses of the weakening lead mules upstream.

Taking a quick gander down over the side, he saw that Rasmussen was still floating aboard the tree bole. A glance upriver showed him the other wagons in good order, none in trouble as they made a staggered, diagonal line downriver toward the west bank. One by one, the Kentucky wagons emerged from the flood-churned ordeal at a sandy bend almost a mile below the start and more than half that below the Trail.

Fargo had his own matters fairly well in hand by now. It wasn't long before he drew within fifteen yards of the west bank, with things going along so swimmingly, so to speak, that he was almost tempted to hope they might make it ashore without further mishap.

When Fargo was less than ten yards from the bank, the teams became remarkably active. They seemed more spirited, not merely striving but also succeeding, noticeably picking up the pace of the outfit. Fargo was not pleased. As soon as he noticed the leaders gaining traction, he knew the cause, and knew he couldn't avoid hitting it.

The wagon hit, nearly catapulting Fargo from

his seat as the Conestoga was jarred and slammed caterwompers.

They had hit a shallow sandbar stretching out into the river. Bars were formed by whim of current and deposit, washed out the next year and regrown elsewhere, no two alike, though many lay invisible on all but calm, clear days. Most bars didn't make good fords. Others were calamitous, such as this one, capable of demolishing a wagon to planks.

The maverick mules slammed the wagon up against it. Right then, however, the wagon was not Fargo's greatest concern. Even while reeling and pitching and choking on splashed water, Fargo tried to keep track of Rasmussen below.

Rasmussen didn't stay below for very long.

From the outset, when the mules first began hauling, the wagon had thrashed within the tight belt of flotsam. The huge tree was still snagged in the wheels, but now there was constant pressure on the wheels to turn, instead of merely sliding along. Strains swiftly began producing shiftings, and chunks of the complicated linkage started to loosen.

There was a doomed man's realization in the brief glimpse Fargo had of Rasmussen. "Swim!" he called, but Rasmussen was beyond hearing. The wagon teetered sideward, bumping harshly. Fargo straightened, only to be tossed again as the wagon lurched over another obstacle, and he went teetering, groping for support while the mules plugged and yanked the wagon onward.

With a crack, the tree tore free from the wheels. It was still loosely enmeshed within the muddle, which was beginning to fragment, separating outward and toward midriver. Rasmussen clung to the tree with a death grip. Then, of a sudden, the whole tangle disengaged. Rasmussen's grasp was wrenched free, and he was thrust rolling from the tree into the river, splashing frantically.

"Swim!" Fargo shouted.

Rasmussen sank. Seconds later, his head bobbed above water farther downstream.

"Swim! Swim to shore!"

Rasmussen's frantic howl carried piercingly. "I can't swim!" Then he was floundering and sinking again among the parting flotsam.

"He can't even wade!" Fargo cursed, leaping from the wagon seat in a shallow, long-skimming dive.

Dazed and gasping, Rasmussen surfaced, only to be caught by the surging current. Fargo swam furiously in an effort to intercept him. He reached out, missed, stroked, and reached again, fingers tightening on the scruff of Rasmussen's shirt, then thrust shoreward. They were halfway there when a snaggle-branched limb reared out of the surface and rammed Rasmussen. Fargo's grasp was torn loose, and the drunk was thrust back into the swirling flow. Fargo made a lunge for him, but he was gone, hurling on downriver.

Fargo speared after him, swimming with the current in a furious effort to intercept Rasmussen. As he closed, Rasmussen, struggling weakly, rolled sluggishly to the surface just ahead of him, then sank. Fargo went under, swimming down. His reaching hands locked on the drowning man, he fought his way to the surface and swung Rasmussen's head clear in a neck hold.

As Fargo began stroking toward the shore, he could see the crazed mules lugging the heavily laden Rasmussen wagon shoreward, preferring dry land to sandbars and needing no driver. Some of the settlers were running down along the bank. A few carried coils of rope, but Fargo figured he wouldn't need hoisting out; he should be ashore by the time the settlers got there. But the current was strong and fighting hard to hold its impetuous grip. As he battled for the bank, Fargo almost lost Rasmussen again before staggering up on the bank.

The first of the men rushed up and helped Fargo turn the limp body of Rasmussen over a deadfall, where the water could drain out of him. More settlers kept coming, grouping about as respiration and life were forced back into the unconscious man. Marshall charged in on his saddler, a *moro* with tan legs, just minutes after Rasmussen revived, hacking and sputtering. The peppery wagon boss fumbled his rein-tying, Fargo noticed, then left it botched as if he was already hot and impatient from delays, and stomped off to brace Rasmussen.

Rasmussen lay recovering on a blanket, wheezing apologetically to Fargo, alongside. "Sorry, I shoulda fessed to you I couldn't swim."

"You should've drowned!" Marshall interrupted, barging in through the cluster of settlers. "You damn fool! You could have put the whole train in danger! Why didn't you do what I told you?"

"Perhaps," Rasmussen conceded, "I'm bullheaded." Slowly he sat up, adding, "But I'm tired of having you make out that you're a better man than me." He coughed, threw up a small quantity of water, and settled down again, his eyes closing, and passed out.

Marshall looked disconcerted. "Maybe God doesn't hate a coward half as much as I figured," he remarked, casting a speculative eye at Rasmussen, who was sleeping, breathing normally. Since Rasmussen wasn't available, Marshall turned on Fargo. "A hell of a reins man you turned out to be. Don't you know anything? Those lead mules could've spun around them roots and gotten all fouled up when you tied the lines and went rooting for Rasmussen's rotgut."

"Hell," Fargo swore, pivoting. "I almost forgot about the stowaway."

A hand caught his shoulder and whirled him. He found himself facing Abel Rasmussen, bristling, snarling, "You trail bum! It was a gift of God the wagon didn't capsize while you left my pa out to drown. What were you doin'? Fixin' yourself a snack?"

Fargo said in a soft drawl, "Nothing in particular, Abel. Just step aside and let me pass."

"I'll step when I get ready!"

Marshall made a growling sound. "Stop it, Rasmussen. Stop it now."

It was too late, of course. No one could stop it now.

"I won't step away," Abel insisted, hard and unyielding. "It's you what oughta step away, Fargo, away'n gone! Instead mouthing off, and mauling decent men and women around here, steppin' in where you ain't wanted."

"The lady," Fargo said quietly, feeling his lips drawing against his teeth, "is perfectly safe from me."

"Oh! So she's not good enough for a damn' rough-scuffer pony scout," Abel said, scowling with righteous indignation. His switch from his father to his gal Julia went smoother than Fargo had thought, but of course that's what Abel was always after, in one way or another. It was all show, Fargo knew—just the routine introducing the main act. "You got a lesson coming, Fargo. I aim to teach you manners."

Abel was pretty shrewd, at that. Even while he was talking, he was charging Fargo, suddenly wading in.

Alert for just such a maneuver, Fargo dodged away. Abel bored after with fists swinging, confident of his brute power, but Fargo was irritated enough by his jealous antagonism to hanker knocking some sense into the farmsteader. Weaving, the Trailsman dipped in under the sledgehammering blows, his long arms reaching out, one hand seizing Abel by the throat of his shirt, the other pistoning a short, looping punch.

Abel tried to wrench loose and dodge aside—a futile struggle. The fist struck the high edge of his jaw and snapped his head at an angle as if he'd hit the end of a hangman's noose. Fargo then freed the shirt with a shove, and Abel stumbled backward.

"Easy," Fargo cautioned, waiting for Abel to get up.

Abel got up, but wasn't easy about it, rushing Fargo with fists windmilling. Fargo sidestepped and rabbit-punched Abel as he went past. Abel dropped again, sliding on his face, rolled over, and rose in a mad scrambling leap.

Fargo ducked, but not in time. A right smashed through his guard, and he felt the salt taste of blood in his mouth from a cut lip, the meaty impact momentarily stunning him. Abel wrapped a strangling arm around his neck and was about to bash his face in with stiff finishers when Fargo butted back, smacking Abel in the nose. Abel staggered, snorting blood from his nostrils, inadvertently lowering his guard and allowing Fargo to catch him behind the ear with a roundhouse punch. With his head twisted around and his legs awry, he was trying to regain his footing when Fargo drummed in, slugging his face, ribs, and belly. Abel's head bounced backward at every brutal contact, and every time it tipped forward, Fargo's fist met it.

Like a blundering, half-wounded buffalo, Abel tried lashing back on the defensive. But Fargo shifted and feinted, pressing his advantage with a relentless compulsion. The impact of his incessantly battering one-two combinations drained the stamina from Abel's knees, and he foundered, looking foggily bewildered. Fargo set his heels, then, and uncorked his right fist from somewhere down around his boots, clobbering Abel smack on the chin.

Abel reeled back, wobbling on buckling legs, and toppled on his butt in a spraddle-legged position, dazed but far from out. Fargo stood waiting, chest heaving, thinking this was a lull, the fight wasn't over.

It was then Julia Talbot showed up, cheeks burning, and halted just aside of them.

Fargo nodded at the girl. "Sorry, Miss Talbot."

"Don't be, Mr. Fargo. Mr. Rasmussen reaped what he sowed."

Rasmussen reared up, blood dribbling from his nose. "Well, it gets me right annoyed, Julie, seeing the way he's always pestering you."

"He never has," she retorted crossly.

With a thin grin, Fargo asked, "You got more complaints?"

Abel swabbed his nose, glaring at Fargo as though running something through his mind. Finally he said, "I'm still keeping my eye on you, and I'll cut you down the first funny move you try."

"You'll kill me dead, wasn't that it?" Fargo's grin died and the blue in his eyes chilled like arctic waters. "I'll take a lot of killing, Abel," he said softly. "Always remember that."

With that, Fargo strode through the gathered settlers, ignoring their stares and murmurous comments as he hurried after Rasmussen's wagon. It had eventually reached shore, the mules having pulled it above the high-water mark where they could graze. He first ran to the rear, opened the tailgate to drain the wagon, then climbed to the boot by the wheel to set the brake. Rear or front, he caught neither sight nor sound of the girl. He made a search, vainly. It was as if the whole incident was a bad dream.

Hap Marshall came stumping up, demanding to know what he'd meant by stowaway. Fargo told him about finding the boy, though not about finding the boy to be a girl, doubting even as he was explaining.

Marshall thought it a hoot, taunting Fargo with scoffs and scorns. No one had seen any kid leave the Rasmussen wagon. But somehow he—she—had left, and soon it was discovered she had not departed empty-handed. Marshall's horse, left virtually unhitched, had easily jerked free and meandered off on its own; there were several men who would swear to that. But the *moro* was not to be found. The tracks led into the timber, where they showed it had been mounted and put at once into a hard gallop.

Marshall ceased laughing.

4

Grudgingly Hap Marshall agreed to lay over for the day.

Fires burned high until late that night, the women drying soaked clothes and durables, the men salvaging what they could of sodden foodstuffs and taking stock of their losses. Fargo tended his horse, which had swum ashore farther downstream and then grazed until he picked him up; other than scratches and a bruised foreleg, the Ovaro seemed in fit shape. Later Fargo rode out as usual to scout the area, taking time for an expanded search in hopes of finding Marshall's horse—with or without the girl—so Marshall would quit belly-aching. He had no success.

Pulling out early next morning, the train left the drizzles behind at the river for a while, which was enough to heighten spirits as the farmsteaders rolled westward along the Overland Trail. The crossing of the Green, the battles with the mud, the Indian alarums, all these were not forgotten, could never be forgotten, but were like harrowing nightmares from which there had been a relieved awakening.

Hap Marshall, brooding over the loss of his horse, rode Fargo instead. And Fargo took it quietly, still pondering who the thief had been, why she'd sneaked a ride rather than hitch a lift across the river. How and when were simpler, he figured; she must have chosen the Rasmussen wagon after studying the train awhile, then during their hectic rush to prepare for the crossing, she would have easily slipped by unnoticed as just another blue-jeaned lad.

Also worth pondering, Fargo reckoned, was the outgrowth of a suggestion to Elaine Talbot. He casually observed that her husband's piebald dray mare was never ridden and needed the exercise. Next day, she and Julia began riding the mare regularly, and lacking a woman's sidesaddle, they straddled the animal wearing his old workpants, which Elaine considered sensible. The settler wives reveled in scandalized shock, then promptly donned their husbands' dungarees with quips about who wore the breeches in the family, although some of them were too robust and hefty to fit on a pair. Fargo, of course, had keen interest in the altering shape of their female uprising.

And, consequently, the Talbots asked Fargo to teach them how to ride astride, man-style. Both were quick and apt, and he enjoyed training them, judging how each in turn rode the mare, bouncing unavoidably in the oversized saddle, straining the seams of denims cut for a lean-flanked man, not their womanly thighs. Watching, Fargo marveled the end effect of his chance remark. Elaine and Julia were plumb uplifting to contemplate asaddle, though if forced to druther, Fargo supposed he'd pick Elaine. She'd rallied back to blooming health—blooming, that is, with the outstanding figure of a woman young enough to be Julia's older sister. Even her smooth, fair face seemed unmarred by age, much less hardship, as she rode tall, her bronze-hued hair now glorious in the sunlight, her cheeks flushed and her warm eyes a-sparkling.

Hers were not the only eyes. Now and again Fargo sensed the impact of staring eyes and found sullen Abel Rasmussen peering from the shadows, his dark eyes beset, his expression fixated. Damn the obsessed lummox! He was building an account that must sooner or later be settled . . . in blood.

All the while they kept following the Trail, along the Muddy, over a roadbed deep-rutted by wheels of bygone pioneers, up Black's Creek, with gracious antelope circling the train in daring curiosity.

Opposite the mouth of Smith's Fork, an eastbound farmer passed them in his dilapidated high-box wagon, pulled by a pair of lumbering plow horses. He kept haranguing to go faster, but it was just as well the stolid team was made for power, not speed, for the wagon was heavily overburdened with people and their possessions, crammed nigh to standing in the bed and hanging precariously over the tailboard and warped side rails. A cheer ran along the line of settler wagons, but it was not echoed by the usual banter from those met en route. Somber-visaged, worried-faced, scared-looking folks erupted shouting in a clamor too confusing to understand, though on occasion someone would manage to clear a few words above the others.

"Turn back while you can!"

"It's war! War to the knife!"

"Hurry and you can make it back to Fort Laramie!"

"Thousands slain! Wagon and stock stolen!"

Soon the yammering babble faded in the wake of the farm wagon's passage, leaving the settlers alarmed without knowing what over. They began fussing and fretting, visiting between wagons and buttonholing Fargo and Marshall with every cockamamy threat their anxious imaginations could scare up. After all, a spine-shuddery fright helped break the monotony.

When Fargo rode alongside, Marshall shifted on his wagon seat and let out a scornful snort. "War! Thousands dead! So they're the sort of craven coyotes that're out here, reading smoke signals out of prairie haze. Bet you one of them thought he seen a feather up yonder a piece and spooked everyone else."

"Assuming they did exaggerate the number killed," Fargo said, "there must have been a train destroyed somewhere ahead on the Trail. Maybe by Paiutes. Wouldn't hurt for you folk to drive with your rifles on your laps. Doubling the night guard and sleeping with one eye—"

"Balderdash. I ain't cowerin' like them yellow fools that just fled by. A man trying to tame this godforsaken country don't grovel, he rides his luck with long spurs when he's winnin'. "

"Damn-fool recklessness wins once in a while, Hap, but more often it loses . . . big."

Marshall scoffed and fell silent. Fargo reined away, aware there was no further use arguing the point. He smiled inwardly when, during the noon stop, he overheard Marshall instructing the company to keep "your weapons handy and your eyes skinned onto the skylines. If I pull into a circle, whip your critters down the flank and close 'er up fast the way Fargo showed us."

Fargo was secretly tickled that the old hard-shell held silent throughout the long afternoon, his eyes alternately searching the brushy reaches of the Trail ahead, the ridge lines—on the right and across the creek to the left, and casting an occasional troubled glance far behind the Trail. Once, when he caught Fargo observing him half-humorously, he growled, "Damned if you ain't got me doin' it, chasin' my shadow an' seein' crawly Injuns in wind-fanned brush."

Toward dusk, seeing they wouldn't make the few miles up the Fork to Fort Bridger, Fargo had Marshall circle the train tightly with all stock inside and set a double night guard. After scouting, he ate supper with Marshall but declined to stay for home brew and cribbage.

"Sorry, Hap. Tonight I'm taking a trip to the fort."

"What for? Word is it's shank-deep in troopers and Mormonites."

"So there's where to go ask what the hubbub's about."

"You're daft! Soldiers are blind liars, and them heretics must be too. They're all itching to skin any fools not of their stripes." Marshall spat, then scoffed, "Naw, I'll wager you and Jim Bridger are personal chums. You'll toss a few drinks with the old fool and learn all about it."

Fargo grinned wryly, for he and Bridger were friendly. "Good idea, Hap," he allowed, "except Bridger's off guiding an expedition up the Yellowstone. I guess I'll just have to run the same risks as other strangers. But don't worry about me, I'll take care of myself."

"Says you," Marshall retorted. "Acts speak louder, and I pegged you soon as we met. More'n likely you'll swell up and play the prize chump over the first army trollop who bats her bustle at you. With your luck, she'll be some general's private baggage, and you'll be carried out feetfirst." Grumbling, Marshall rose from the cook fire. "Someone's gotta keep you on the straight and narrow, else we'll never see California. C'mon, I'll mooch a horse and gear. Maybe I'll even find mine down there somewhere."

Soon, with Marshall aboard a hock-scarred splotched paint, they left for the fort. The paint proved to be as cantankerous as its rider, and for a while tried to enliven the trip, but in the end it was outperversed by Marshall and gave up the notion of throwing him, settling instead for an uneasy truce. The rest of their journey was uneventful.

When first sighted, gloomy Fort Bridger was a black bulk looming against the softer dark of the night sky. The base was lost in a murk that smeared on into the landscape, concealing the tents and hovels that Fargo recalled were clustered by the fort, though he did spot a few dots of lamplight. The fort itself showed no lights, save for a weak glow hovering above the roofline, a reflection radiating from whatever lanterns were lit within the enclosing palisade.

A quarter-mile east, the Mormon post flared like a beacon, lamplight streaming from every window. As Fargo turned to head toward the post, Hap Marshall barked in protest.

"You took leave of your senses? If you ain't a natural-born nincompoop, stay away from that den and all their dens of iniquities!"

"Nuts. It's a trade post like any other, a gathering spot for news."

"Mormon news, dunce! I boned up on 'em before the trek, an' they're a caution. Mumbo-jumbo doctrines and a special kind o' God Almighty who orders 'em to enslave women and murder men—even their men who don't see eye to eye with the leaders, and non-Mormon prisoners who refuse conversion. And they have to marry a herd of wives, worst curse ever, making a man suffer damnation till he dies and can slack off in hell. If you ain't hoodooed by their black magic, they'll plain lambaste you into joining. Or dying."

With a faint grin, Fargo shook his head. "Yes, there are bad Mormons, just like there're bad eggs in every religion. Too often only the bad stuff gets told, since it makes hotter stories. But I've visited that post before and dealt with the Mormons, Hap, and it isn't their habit to force their beliefs on anyone."

"All right, go there, you double-damned cretin. And while you're taking your trip to the netherworld, I'll learn where the feathers was seen that scared those fool farmers. Be back in an hour so I can give your remains a decent burial." He spurred on, flinging back across his shoulder, "If you need help, lift Kentucky's Cumberland Hunting Call."

Whatever that was, Fargo thought as he set off at a lope.

The Mormon post consisted of the large log cabin of the post store, blacksmith and supply shacks, and a lean-to stable with adjoining pole corrals, all grouped facing around a clearing. Established by a stern duck named M. Lehi, it had been part of a chain of Mormon ventures that were linked cooperatively, spurning non-Mormon business—Fargo had learned this from Bridger, who'd been incensed by the church's "exclusive" policies. It had been run by Lehi until his death—a murder charged to Indians by most, to Bridger men by the Mormons—then was taken over by non-Mormons, partners Magee and Wayland, who in due course turned it into more of a sutler's operation. Yet it kept being called the Mormon post, partly from habit, mostly from the Mormons' continuing trade. They shunned the fort save in dire emergencies, especially since '57, when troopers were first stationed there and Bridger guided Colonel Johnston's offensive against the Mormons. Of course, Bridger considered his help retaliation for the business freeze-out.

Fargo tied his pinto to an already crowded rack and pushed confidently into the post. A long aisleway had full-length counters, flanked by an island of piled goods in the middle. Halfway was a potbellied stove, fired against the evening chill, with eighteen or so men clustering around. A dozen, Fargo estimated, were strapping laborers mostly in their twenties—Mormons surely, or they would have been over at Fort Bridger. The others were bleach-eyed, stubble-faced jaspers lounging with studied ease and tied-down guns—backtrail riffraff who'd steer shy of forts or most any place reasonably large and law-abiding. The two groups weren't really together or even mingling much, but there wasn't enough room around the stove to avoid one another.

Fargo listened to their drawling laughter and the spasmodic profanity from the gun thugs, but didn't catch anything of interest. As Fargo drew nearer, their talk faded off into a tense hush. The air swam with cigar smoke, but none held a cigar. One of the Mormons toed a jug under the stove. Here were earmarks of Brigham's lost lambs, men who had swapped their faith for material pleasure. Upon reaching the stove area, Fargo said, " 'Evening," but they didn't respond, not a word, not a nod. Right then and there Skye suspected he may've stepped accidentally into trouble. Even the orneriest polecat would have acknowledged his greeting, if only rudely.

Scanning, Fargo glimpsed Magee and Wayland on the other side of the stove. The scoundrel partners had the MW Ranch in northern Arizona, and somehow managed to make it pay without spending much time there, leaving them free to move from shady deal to deal. Fargo had chanced upon them occasionally, every time catching one or both in some petty larceny, coming mighty close to showdowns and not wildly enthused about tackling them together.

Weasel-faced Magee, who claimed to have been a Pony Express rider, packed an Arkansas toothpick, needle-pointed and double-edged, and a Beals .31 revolver in a shoulder holster. Wayland stood six-three at two-fifty, all big bone and hard meat. His tow hair was graying, his face had a battered look and his eyes were pale gray, and he could clean out a saloon full of men in a knock-down-and-drag-out. During such brawls, nobody paid much attention to Magee, who'd dart among the fighters and hamstring them. He could cut the legs from under a man and be out of reach before the man hit the floor, and he was as fast with his pistol as with his knife. Magee and Wayland were a tough pair to beat.

The silence stretched. Fargo was in no hurry to break it, and was wondering who'd crack first, when outside, clear and sharp, sounded the lingering notes of trumpeted taps. If this puzzled Fargo, it startled the Mormon bunch. The gunmen didn't turn a hair, not looking mean or pleased or anything in between, just case-hardened indifferent. Not so the Mormons, Fargo reading nervousness in their uneasy eyes and restless fidgits.

He asked, "How come, guys? Jim Bridger calling curfew for the Indians now?"

They averted their eyes. One sunburnt, buck-toothed character, though, grimaced at Fargo with a mix of disdain and righteous indignation. "It's the non-Mormon war cry against Deseret," he proclaimed, and it was then the gunmen began chugalugging their drinks and leaving. The Mormon scarcely noticed, tirading on, "Let them try to profane our mountains and valleys. God upholds our banners. Zion's hosts spring to defend the Promised Land and force the recognition of Deseret by—" He broke off, stooping for the jug by his feet.

Fargo moved, shouldering through the flock around the stove and on back to Magee and Wayland. "Friendly cusses," he remarked after nodding hello.

Wayland chortled boozily; he was slouched in a decrepit armchair, nursing a bottle of whiskey. Standing closeby, wiping his hands on a towel, Magee frowned and snapped, "They'll smile real purty soon's you go."

"So will I, Magee. Any word of trouble on west?"

"Nope."

"We caught scare talk coming in. Twice while out scouting, I crossed paths of mounted Shoshone. There'd been no squaws with them. Might have been hunting parties. Then again they might have been wearing war paint."

"Then again your head might've been stuffed up your ass. Now, get!"

"I heard tell," Wayland declared, grinning lopsidedly. And Fargo smelled a setup coming, with a nasty catch hooked in it. "Wasn't no Injun massacre, Fargo, was a slaughterous rampage by them Danites, them Avenging Angels. Scuttlebutt has it they killed everyone found guilty o' Trail outrages, which o' course means everyone they found. Nary any o' us heathens left alive. Just like they'd supposedly wiped out them Jack Mormons that settled Blockade Valley a while back, every except one, the Jack Mormon who led 'em there. Jophiel Ladderer."

Around the stove, the Mormons passed the jug and drank quietly, enmity hardening their faces and chilling their eyes. Wayland was after them, not him, Fargo realized; was sticking it to them on a drunken whim, by the sound of his talk.

"Uh-huh, Deacon Jophiel Ladderer. Too tough to die. Laid up on a rimrock, and when the valley battle was over, and what Danites were left rode Injun-file through the narrow pass below the rimrock, Jophiel Ladderer shot the first and last Danite in line. Shot 'em and their horses dead to block the narrow pass at both ends. Then he killed the Danites trapped in the middle, cut 'em down like settin' hens. That left Jophiel Ladderer sole owner of Blockade Valley. And in addition to his own two-three-four wives, Jophiel Ladderer fell heir to the plural wives of them other Jack Mormons. Now ain't that slay you?"

Wayland roared with drunken laughter, slapped his huge thigh, and took a long pull on his bottle. His laughter died as the Mormons drained their jug, and one of them raised it in a mock salute, toasting him. "Here's to the oldest wolf on the plains, Gentile. May he live to see you all dangling like tassels from the ends of stout ropes." He tossed the jug aside and they all strode out in a body.

Wayland sobered some more under the beady black eyes of Magee, who said, "You beller to loud."

Nor had Fargo joined in Wayland's bellowing laughter. Easy as it was for him to grin at anything like a joke, he could find nothing to even smile about. He moved doorward.

Behind him, Magee called snidely, "Goin' so soon, Fargo?"

Fargo turned, smiling affably. "Maybe not just yet. Got some tobacco or a cigar like the boys were smoking against Church orders?"

"Got nuthin' for you, not even the sweat off my balls."

"Hell, no, save your sweat. You start giving or selling it, you won't have any for flavoring your bootleg pissbrew." Fargo opened the door and went out.

Crossing the porch, descending the log steps, he sensed the leap of a shadow from his right. Wheeling, he drew his revolver and met the attack with a smashing gun barrel. There were two more and Fargo hurtled at them. One caught his gun arm. Bootsteps thudded on the porch floor. Men landed crushingly atop his shoulders, clubbing him with hardwood truncheons, wrenching his revolver away, and battering his skull.

Fargo staggered for footing, bracing his legs wide and straining to keep from flattening. He parried a punch with an uppercut and slammed a knee into another attacker's groin, while chopping the side of his hand across someone else's face, cracking bones. He snagged two attackers, one in each fist, and bashed their heads together. Before they had fallen, he was mauling yet another man, fighting to break out. But this was an experienced brawler who refused to be taken easily.

Inevitably the attackers engulfed Fargo. Sweaty, dirty,

angry at having to exert themselves, they surged, arms seizing and wooden clubs smashing. Fargo stumbled to his knees, then rolled as they swarmed like wolves on a hamstrung bull. He twisted, broke their holds, clubbing them with their own sticks, but it was hopeless. They pinned his legs. They choked him. He got clobbered in a vise of three men, and the rest of their gang seemed to all land knuckles and clubs simultaneously.

Fargo hit the dirt, snuffed like a candle.

5

Fargo came to with dry tongue, throbbing skull, and the taste of blood in his mouth. Demon lances stabbed his eyes as he opened them to the flare of two tallow dips on a table of roughly adzed logs. Beyond that bright patch was all a muddy blur, his vision not yet fully restored, but that was all right, because he hadn't recovered all of his wits yet, either.

Meager as they were, his motions drew attention. He could hear a mutter of voices die away, and began to discern outlines of men moving about as increasingly his surroundings gained shape and sense. He saw he was in a small blacksmith's shop, no doubt the smithy shack on the Mormon post, along with a dozen beefy men who looked mighty familiar. The last time he'd seen them clearly, they were walking out on Wayland's store; since then, most appeared to have gotten bruised and lacerated, a few limped, and some had their noses and mouths and other features extensively rearranged, though Fargo had no real trouble recognizing them. By now they surely knew who he was, for everything in his pockets and saddlebags, including weapons, had been dumped on the table. He sat at the table, trussed to a chair with his hands behind its high back, his ankles lashed to its bottom rung, and his torso bound to the frame as if they'd tried to sew him in the chair.

A score of eyes glared at him, the most virulent of

them belonging to the man seated across the table from him, between the candles. It was the firebrand who'd railed against the non-Mormon war cry, and now he was trying his damnedest to be in charge. He knew a few tricks, such as sitting with his back against a wall, close enough to a corner to block others from clustering around. It might have worked better if the room's only window hadn't been right behind him, the oiled pane making little slapping noises as a night breeze puffed against it. And arranging it so that candles framed him was a bit thick. He'd been left in charge, Fargo reckoned—the sort put in charge when everybody who should be in charge has to be away.

It didn't make him any less dangerous, and maybe more so.

"High time, Skye Fargo. My brother officers get restless."

"Don't let me keep you waiting," Fargo grumped.

"Hardly. We're only awaiting our captain before court-martialing you."

"Trial?" Fargo shifted to ease his cramped limbs. "For what, then?"

Instead of an answer, the Mormon asked, "When are you to meet?"

Thinking of Hap, Fargo lied, "No meet, we're on our own. That way I can stay out late."

"Don't lie, Fargo, we're not nitwits. Whether you split or stay together, you still must meet once more. Now, where is your rendezvous?"

"Must be my ears going bad from all those head blows. You can't have said what I thought I heard you say, 'cause none of it made any sense."

"Don't play the fool either, you're no nitwit. It took brains and cunning to get hired on the only train fitting your timetable, and to keep it on schedule. Your cover was good, too. Just not quite good enough.

Now, while it's still easy, tell us when and where you're set to rendezvous?"

Fargo licked his lips. They were watching him with a strange mixture of eagerness and cold suspicion, and he didn't know what to tell them, so he stalled. "Nuts. I'll save my say for the trial. What are the charges?"

"Deceiving a virgin daughter of Zion into the harlotry of Babylon. Grand larceny, too. For your offenses, you face a court-martial of the Phalanx of Gideon. For your guilt, you pay the extreme penalty. Understand?"

Fargo nodded. Nothing else he understood, but he could read the verdict clearly in the Mormon's eyes. The extreme penalty in Mormon Utah was death by hanging. He could feel his innards clenching, knotting, though not from any vast horror of the hangman's noose. Wasn't one of his druthers, but he was churned more by his helplessness to do or say anything to prevent it.

"I don't know a lot about the Mormons," he began in a controlled voice. "I figure my beliefs are my own business, and I don't meddle with the other man's ways of worship." His taut nerves began to snap, then, his eyes a frigid blue and his voice thickening with frustration and exasperation. "There's no worship to your trial. No justice, either, in a court run by bushwhackers. Nothing honorable in judges and juries of cowards, who hide behind rocks and brush by night. You hang me, it's lynching. All your tying it in with your psalm-singing and preaching doesn't make it God's law. It's no law. It's murder, by murderers with the piety of jackals."

"Good and evil both stem from Jehovah that worketh all things for His greater glory."

Here, Fargo thought, was fanaticism that blunted fear. They would kill him unless Hap broke it up, and that was but a faint hope. And how could the wagon master handle a dozen armed men, even if he did find the shed?

The answer was an almost imperceptible movement behind the leader. Fargo was directly facing the window and caught the ripple, but for the others, the table and the man concealed it. A revolver barrel inched through a rent in the oiled pane, and Fargo averted his eyes so they might not read warning in them.

The Mormon stiffened when the gun muzzle jabbed his back, his expression dropping to a sort of sickly despair. Fargo was grinning, and grinned wider when a whispered voice that only Fargo and his accuser could hear said, "You die first. Anything goes wrong, anybody gets smart, you get the first shot. Now, have him untied."

In a throttled voice, the leader ordered the two men nearest to Fargo to cut him loose, winging the excuse that it was part of his investigation needed for the court-martial. The men looked suspicious, but went right to work on the knots with sharp blades. A moment later Fargo stood up on crampy legs, trying to rub a little feeling into his numbed fingers, and hastened to clean the table of his belongings, stuffing his saddlebags. That was all of his riding gear in the cabin, and he wondered what they'd done with the rest, and with his Ovaro. He worked swiftly but with no sudden, threatening moves, everyone watching him without anyone knowing what to be looking for. They soon would, he figured; the next part was up to him.

Slinging the bags on his shoulder, he headed for the man at the window, who glared reproachfully, murder hooding his eyes. Tough—he'd put himself in this position and had no one else to blame. Fargo took over as the revolver at the window was withdrawn through the oiled pane, stabbing his own Colt into the man's spine with one hand while pulling him upright and close as a shield. The saddlebags made it more cumbersome, but it had to be done, now, and he started for the door in a fast lockstep, loud with determination and ruthlessness.

"Everybody, lift hands! I mean it, get them up. Any of you think you're heroes, think again. I'll shoot this brother officer of yours through his spine, and I'll blow your brains out too. I've got nothing to lose. You, there, open the door!"

"Hell I will! We got you trapped in here!"

A shot blasted through the oiled pane behind Fargo. The defiant Mormon let out a howl and clapped a hand over his left ear—or where the ear had been.

Shifting a glance, Fargo glimpsed the filmy shape behind the rent pane, features indistinct, then scanned the room, scowling.

"I got *you* trapped, you mean," he snarled. "The place's surrounded by my crew. You want more proof? Who's eager to die? Now, get that door open!"

They got the door open.

"Make way. I'm taking him with me." Fargo backed outside, forcing the man to back with him. "He won't get hurt, not if he stays a good boy. So don't worry; everybody stay calm and nobody ends up dead."

He booted the door shut. The noise of its slam was still reverberating when the voice called to him from the darkness at the left end—the side with the window. "This way! You first, Mormon, hurry! Around this way!"

The Mormon trotted toward the corner, Fargo a few paces behind, working out the last few kinks in his legs. The Mormon went around the corner, and Fargo, coming around, heard a hollow *thwunk* and then saw the man on the ground, inert but groaning. A voice said, "Stunned, is all. Come on, I've got your horse fetched back here." And a shadow led the way.

Fargo hastened after, around the rear corner to

where his Ovaro and a saddled moleskin grulla waited. His horse was full geared save for the saddlebags, which he now attached hurriedly, followed by a swift check of the cinches. Mounting, he sent the pinto leaping after the other. The log buildings and pole corrals of the post were fast put behind them. They plunged into a stand of trees as a vengeful roar swelled from the blacksmith shack. Raging men emerged like aroused ants, their gun flashes streaking the night. Five men were quickly mounted and galloping into the timber.

Fargo, dogging after the grulla, plunged through gloomy woods, shrouded culverts, and bouldered pockets on a route that concealed them from view. That meant the rider ahead wasn't Hap Marshall, who'd never been hereabouts before. The rider was a dark-clad huddle atop a moleskin-hued phantom, that's all Fargo knew, and that wasn't enough. Instead of wisely cutting for the fort, he continued to follow blindly on a circuitous course that brought him at length to Black's Creek, behind the jutting promontory that hid them from the posts.

The rider halted at the creek, dismounting. A moment later Fargo pulled up by the watering grulla and saw the rider crouching a few yards downstream, scooping a drink. The rider, casting a glance at Fargo, straightened and headed back along the bank. Fargo swung from the saddle, stepping clear of the horses and into the open, feeling he'd had enough surprises for one night. He got one anyway when they met.

"You!"

"Well, a dried-off, patched-up, different-clothes me," she replied pertly, tilting back her scruffy hat from burnished red hair. She'd changed from the boy's duds into a man's range garb, and wearing it seemed to have changed her. That was the impression Fargo got, anyway—a gut sense that she was no longer the half-drowned whelp he'd salvaged in the dim confines of Rasmussen's wagon. What had passed for a lad had grown up, grown older. What had hidden as a girl had matured into a young woman, slender, with a straight, delicately chiseled nose, firm chin, and red lips quirked in a smile as she added, "All of me owes you a thank-you. So, thank you. Now your debt is paid in full."

"Debt?"

"You saved me. What goes 'round, comes 'round, and it just so happened I was in the rear stockroom of the post store when you entered. After the fight, I bided my time, hoping for a chance to rescue you from those men."

"Tit for tat, eh?"

"Yes, and we're lucky it didn't end up a bust." She paused reflectively, her green eyes storm-cloudy as if, turning inward, she was churning a tempest. Low and growly, she mulled aloud, "That's a maverick group, that Phalanx of Gideon. They're Zealots, more faithful Mormons than I am. But nothing can excuse their wanton murder and banditry, or what they did to . . ." She choked off, her last thought too private or painful to utter, and stared up at Fargo with a probing intensity. "I want you to take me away—take me with you."

Fargo started, searched vainly for the lie in her eyes. "You just said you're Mormon. You—you'd leave this all?"

"I already left Zion. I can't go back yet, I've things to do." She held his gaze with her eyes—dark, verdant maelstroms now, drawing him in. "I'm asking too much. You'd risk your entire train. If they saw me, or heard I was aboard, they'd probably jump the train. Don't underestimate them. They drill and train like soldiers."

"I know; I heard the taps," Fargo said, figuring it

all was adding up to something stinko brewing around here. That harum-scarum farm wagon; the Phalanx of Gideon with its loony charges and lethal habits; and this female finagler who, to go by her dark innuendos, had a lot of dead cats tied to her apron strings. Still, if there were trouble, he wanted to know what to expect.

"You're right, you're asking a lot. Now, I don't know who you are or—"

"Rachel—"

"Or anything about you, Rachel. But I'll call your bluff. From what little I've picked up so far, I'd say the train runs the risk of being attacked in any case. The settlers aren't asleep. They're Kentucky riflemen, sharp country hunters. The women know bullet-molding and gun-loading, and the kids can pass weapons. But the wagon boss hasn't taken kindly to tagalongs since the last one stole his saddler."

"I turned the horse in at the fort livery." She moved close now in the darkness, and Fargo could hear her quick breathing. "Here, take this. It's the money belt."

"Now I know you're joshing."

"I'm serious, dead serious. They're watching for me everywhere, know I'm carrying it, and now they know I'm hereabouts. They mustn't get the belt." Her voice came to him urgently, and their fingers groped and met. "Take it as a precaution. If I . . . we're separated, you go on, and I'll catch up with the train."

Her hands had been cold as ice, trembling, and Fargo warmed them in his. And then she was in his arms and his mouth found hers in the dark, and then her arms were around his neck and there was fear and desperation and perhaps passion in the fierceness of her kiss. Presently she slid from his arms and told him in an unsteady voice to buckle on the money belt.

"They will kill you," she whispered, so close to him that her breath fanned his face. "If they catch us."

"Let them try."

"God teach you fear." Turning, she hastened for the horses.

They were soon asaddle, loping straight toward a mote of tall cottonwoods fringing the creek. Fargo, with Rachel holding the lead, was carried along the west flank of a slope, climbing. They skirted the rim and cut a far slope and swung on a course that would eventually bring them to Fort Bridger. Single-file they rode through a rocky cleft lined with thick brush and huge boulders, Fargo rode right behind her now, his revolver in his hand.

"Hold up!" The flat-toned voice cracked like a pistol across the night's black shadows from behind the brush and boulders.

With a startled cry, she reined in sharply. "Don't!" she called out. "Don't shoot!"

The laugh that came from behind the brush and boulders was short and mirthless. "The daughter of Jophiel Ladderer should know the Law!"

"Kill him"—the girl's voice was brittle—"and I'll force you to shoot me. Or I'll kill myself. Give him his right to live, to ride on his way, and I swear to turn back with you and abide by the Law. But kill this innocent man and I will die with him. That I swear to God!"

Fargo, having no choice but to haul up with her, crowded his horse close against her, peering into the thick black shadows, ready to shoot.

"Don't make that mistake," Rachel cautioned. "Killing is his trade—he wants the chance to murder you. Let me do this. Believe in me. It's our only chance."

Again came that flat-toned laugh from the thick shadows, and now it had a deadlier sound. Fargo had his share of a man's fighting guts, and if there had been the fraction of a chance, he would have taken the risk. But the man was hidden, he was not, and Rachel was smack in open line of fire.

"Ride on, sinner," sounded a flat voice. "Ride on alone."

"Go," Rachel cried. "In God's name go, before you're dead and I die with your blood on my soul. God keep you always. Go!"

She slashed the rump flank of Fargo's horse with her rawhide quirt. The big Ovaro lunged, and Skye Fargo heard that flat-toned laugh echoing back and forth as it followed him through the high, rock-walled pass.

6

Every sense alert, Fargo rode on toward Fort Bridger. Though he could see and hear nothing, he listened to his nagging sense of alarm.

Galling anger made him almost turn back, to somehow track down that laughing bastard and see who laughed last. But a deeper, colder rage checked his rash impulse. Odds were the man had others with him, and getting to Rachel fast enough to get her back alive would be damn tough. And it could well backfire, jeopardizing her chance to escape and catch up with the train, which was how she wanted and planned to handle it.

Beyond the immediate threat to Rachel, moreover, there was the growing danger to folks living and traveling in this area. The fort should be alerted and the wagon train needed to be warned. Dashing after Rachel might well give the phalanx time to plunder and butcher others. Believe in me, Rachel had pleaded. Well, he'd keep the faith for a short while, anyway. He had to.

Coming upon the wagon road that led to the fort, Fargo rode up the trough and rounded the long point, approaching the dark log walls with eyes raking the gloom. He gauged the hour as midnight, wondering if Marshall had returned to the train, hoping he hadn't.

The gates of the post stood open, unguarded. Riding inside, Fargo crossed the trading square with its rimming shelf for kneeling riflemen during attack. Dismounting before a lighted entrance that screamed saloon, he glanced along the rail while tying his horse and spotted Marshall's stolen *moro* standing beside the borrowed paint.

Inside, the joint swam with smoke, reeked of liquor, was filthy. There was a smattering of patrons—a crew of trailhands, for the most part—but no troopers and no Hap Marshall.

The barkeep roused as Fargo neared. "What's yours, neighbor?"

"Do you know where Hap Marshall went?"

"Stringy ol' blister with sandy goat whiskers?"

"Yes, that fits him."

"He ain't left; he's in yonder, playing cards." The barkeep jerked his head toward the rear door. "Go on in. They won't take more than your shirt."

The rear door opened into a small, square backroom. Four men sat at a poker table lighted by burned-down candles, three of them appearing to be more trailhands, and a cackling Hap Marshall laying down a winning hand.

"Bluffed you again!" Marshall clawed in the pot, turning toward the opening door. "Just in time, Fargo. C'mon, boys, cough up for your next hand."

The disgruntled losers anted in; one asking Fargo, "How'd this warthog learn to play cards, as a river pirate?"

"Naw, some little old lady showed him, late last week."

Marshall looked affronted. "I'll have you know, sirs, in Kentucky a boy finds manhood in the first six-pistol he buys with poker winnin's."

"*Kentucky!*" The three players reared to their feet, scowling.

"Kentucky," Marshall repeated. "Why, you got a problem with that?"

"We got no use for Kentuckians," another one snapped. "An' we'll back said remark with guns, knives, or bullwhips!"

Fargo began, "Now, wait—"

Revolvers whipped into calloused palms. The first man said, "We done waited. Now, outside."

Gunbarrels prodding, Marshall and Fargo were marched out into the main saloon, the other men quickly gathering around. Fargo returned their scrutiny, trying to figure the reason for their antagonism, his eyes singling out a brown-bearded bruiser who appeared to be their crew chief.

Marshall wasn't called Hap because of a sunny disposition. "Why, you lizard-eatin' coyotes, I've a right to know why I've turned into poison so dang fast! Do I have to yank on your tongues to hear tell?"

A menacing laugh started to rumble in the crew chief's chest. "Talk's cheap. However, there's good solid ways to come to an understandin'. 'Course it got to test a man's worth, and you ain't no test." He eyed Fargo, then drawled, "Folks call me Grizzly. Just plain Grizzly Jim Jones."

"Fargo, Skye Fargo."

"Stay out of it, Skye," Marshall snapped. "I'm the Kentuckian."

"And this feller's siding with you," Jones retorted, leveling a knobby finger at Fargo. "I'm right handy at sparring, and I'm hankering for some exercise. If you feel like obliging me, Fargo, I'll lay you a side bet. Whip me, and what grievances me and my crew got against Kentuckyites are squared. Now, if I whip you, that's the beginning, not the ending."

Fargo's eyes had begun to narrow, for he had read what was in the brute's mind. He was peeling off his weapons before the other finished speaking, handing them to a protesting Marshall with a testy "Cork it, before you dig us any deeper with your mouth."

A gleam of admiration came into Grizzly Jones' eyes as he saw the ripple of muscles beneath Fargo's shirt. "Glory be," he said, chuckling, "I may get a little exercise at that!"

He rushed on the remark, hoping to catch Fargo off guard, and he almost succeeded. The Trailsman swayed desperately aside as the big man roared past. Once in the Sierras he'd seen a brown grizzly crush the life from a prospector, and the horrible picture floated before his eyes now. Jones, he realized, was strong enough to do the same thing in a clinch.

The bartender was shouting querulously, but was ignored as Jones pivoted and lunged toward Fargo again. This time Fargo did not wait for him, but closed the space between them and put all his weight behind the left fist he buried almost wrist-deep in Jones' gut. Jones humped forward. Fargo swung his right straight into the brute's bearded chin. Jones' head snapped back, but one flailing pawlike hand smashed out with all the lightning of a mountain bear's thrust.

Fargo felt himself flung sidewise, his legs slewing out from under him. Dimly he saw Jones rushing yet again, bellowing out the words, "Here comes the payoff for the killing your sneaky countrymen have done! I hope the dead in hell are watchin' this!"

"Tromp him through the floor!" one of the hands hooted. "Maybe it'll teach these damned Kentuckians to keep hombres like Olin Karnes at home!"

Olin Karnes! Through the roaring in his head, Fargo heard the name, and it stung him like a lash from a whip. Karnes! Grizzly Jim Jones was not the only one who had a score to settle with that man.

The thought brought Fargo to his feet. His fists rapiered out, and the sound of their strike was like a cleaver slapping meat. The blows stopped Jones, and Fargo slid away from his clutching hands. Jones' eyes were swelling almost shut, and his lips were cracked and puffy. He was breathing hard, through a bleeding nose, snuffling, "Stand still an' fight! This ain't no runnin' match!"

And this time Fargo did. "I got two punches left," he taunted huskily. "Come and get them, if you want them."

"And more," Jones roared. He came lunging in again, spitting blood.

Fargo set himself to meet the rush, and he knew he had told the truth. His arms felt leaden, and two blows were about all he did have left to muster. If they didn't stop Jones for good, Jones would trample the life from between his ribs. He ducked a blow and buried his left in the Jones solar plexus again. The fist hurt. Fargo heard Jones' gasp of agony. He stepped back as the other doubled forward, and brought up a sledging right to the man's bearded chin.

This time Jones' head did not snap back. He was falling too fast for that. Out before he touched the floor, Grizzly Jim crumpled in a heap at Fargo's boots. Through the pound of blood in his ears, he heard Marshall crowing.

"There's your overgrown ox, boys, stiffer than a Kentucky ham!"

Fargo wiped his eyes with the back of his hand. "Shut the hell up," he snapped through battered lips, taking back his weapons. "If Grizzly Jones had ever got his hands on me once, you'd be carting me back to camp in chunks."

"An' what Grizzly Jim promised, we'll stick to," one of the trailhands said heartily. "Guess it calls for a drink. Where's the barkeep?"

"Ran out of here squawking," another hand said, going behind the counter to liberate a bottle.

Jones stirred, then, and sat up with bleary eyes and a hand checking his jawbone. "Ain't nothing wrong with a Kentuckian who can fight like that," he remarked approvingly, and took a gurgling snort of whiskey.

"I'm not from Kentucky," Fargo said as the bottle was passed to him. His body ached and throbbed in a dozen places, but a liberal dosage of painkiller helped, and he continued, "And don't be too sure Olin Karnes is, either. Hap and me, and the rest of our train know of Karnes. He deserted a wagon west of the Platte. Left a man and two women alone. The Dakotas got Sam Talbot, but we drove them off in time to save his wife and daughter. They're from Missouri, and according to them, they joined the Karnes' train because Karnes claimed to be from Missouri."

Jones shook his head. "Well, that's a horse on me," he allowed, rearing to his feet. "We were running a sizable drive of cattle over to the valley of the Great Salt Lake when we chanced into Karnes and his train. Fifty men from Kentucky is what we were told they were. We had some Mexicans in the crew, and suddenly they vamoosed. The next night, rustlers came blasting through the camp and stampeded the herd. Shot up our nighthawks and a handful of others asleep, and by the time we got ourselves pieced together and after 'em, they were long out of sight. We don't know the territory all that good, and pretty soon we lost their tracks."

He paused and lit a stubby pipe. When it was drawing properly, Jones continued, "We came here to report the rustling, not that much could be done. And we couldn't prove it was Karnes. But we ran across one of the Mexicans, and he told us why they'd got scared and quit. Karnes' men told them paisanos that Mormons killed Mexicans on sight, which is a load of horseshit. So you can see why we kinda got hot—"

The front door of the saloon burst open. In stormed the bartender, a handful of troopers, and a corporal, the officer on night-guard duty, Fargo suspected. The corporal glared at the bartender. "Okay, where's the riot?"

"They were brawlin' when I left," the barkeep argued.

"Not us," Jones denied devoutly. "We were singing our favorite hymns when he bolted outta here screamin'. Maybe he's been sampling his own wares."

Swearing, the corporal made ready to leave with his squad. Fargo intervened, reporting the evening's events at the Mormon post without betraying the identity of his rescuer. His news stirred an outburst of babbling.

"Danite Avengin' Angels?" the corporal asked Fargo.

"No. There haven't been Danites since the Mormon Church disbanded and outlawed them fifty years ago," Fargo answered. "The stories persist since Danites make great excuses to blame crimes on. And like every religion, the Mormons suffer a certain small number of hotblood fanatics who turn renegade, like this Phalanx of Gideon. Their God-given missions all seem to sound about the same."

The corporal nodded. "Maybe so, maybe so. Our intelligence hasn't supplied a name or the roots of the gang, but has warned us one's been raiding ranches and wagon trains, and might be fool enough to attack here. If they do, Washington might dispatch an expedition into Mormon country, like Johnston's in '57 to quell the rebellion. He got bumped to brigadier general for it." The corporal brightened, young enough to savor the lure of adventure and promotion. "I think the result could well clear the air for all concerned. I'm happy you escaped, Mr. Fargo, and appreciate your information. I'll most definitely pass it on . . ." He paused, starting. A faint sound entered the saloon, not unlike the breaking of a stick. "What was that?"

Through the silence came a far, thin yell and the blasting of guns in the night. Then another sound, impossible to mistake—the rumbling rataplan of a stampeding horse herd.

"The stock!" Troopers leaped to the door, the corporal following. Behind them tumbled Jones and his trail crew. Marshall swung an astonished visage at Fargo. "You think that bunch that cornered you would dare to—"

"Somebody's daring, Hap. And we better get out of here and look after our own stock." He hurried for the door, adding, "I see you recovered your horse."

Hippering alongside, Marshall responded with a querulous grunt. "Yeah, I was asking 'round, and danged if it didn't get left at the stables. I almost didn't get it back, either. Jehosafat, did that hostler charge for corralin'."

They entered the trading ground, where men were bursting from their sleeping quarters, streaking gatewards. From the army camp came a constantly swelling tumult, overridden by the short sharp notes of the trumpet blowing alert.

Fargo untied his horse and swung to the saddle. Marshall took time to pick up the paint, then mounted his moro and they broke for the gate. But no sooner had they charged through the entrance to the compound than they reined in abruptly, and sat there viewing the confusion.

Half-clad troopers and teamsters, barely awake, were answering the frantic piping of the trumpeter, pulling on their clothes as they dashed for the holding ground across the creek. There, the panicked stock drew away toward the north, where the lack of rifle fire suggested an absence of targets. From the post corrals, adjoining the main enclosure on the south, came the mounted partisans of Jim Bridger, rough, tough old-timers who had combed the wilderness for beaver plews. Pioneers without a calling, who now hunted a little, set a few traps to keep their hands in and lived off the generous bounty of their more fortunate trap-line brethren. By ones and twos they quirted and spurred after the stampeding army horses, brandishing long rifles, uttering sharp, wild Blackfoot yells.

Even as Fargo watched, the scene changed. Suddenly the lines of tents and wagons stood alone, untenanted, and the tumult faded in the distance. Hap Marshall came up to join Fargo and behind him were the barkeep and other post menials. Queries ran thick and fast.

And before anybody could suggest an answer, it came, clear and lurid. A tongue of flame licked from a wagon top, another from a tent. Fargo yelled, "Fire!" and launched his Ovaro into gallop. His revolver came to his hand, and when the light of the growing conflagration showed him a darting shadow, he leveled and fired. The shadow fell, writhed, and got up to be swallowed in the flame-tinted smoke that boiled and swirled through the camp.

Scorning the risk of being shot off his horse by the renegades, Fargo dashed in among the wagons, realizing only then that he alone was helpless to avert the catastrophe, or even to attempt salvage. The stench of burning grease was nauseating and it served to emphasize in his mind how cleverly led and well organized were the attackers. Every wagon was already blazing too fiercely to permit a man to enter. Every tent was wreathed in spiraling flames. The renegades had stampeded the horses in order to draw the defense from the camp. Then, almost without being glimpsed, they had splashed melted tallow on the canvas shelters and applied the torch. The camp was doomed.

The troopers came charging back, reacting to the order of some bull-voiced sergeant. Swiftly they formed a bucket brigade that passed up water from the creek in a vain attempt to save the running gear of the wagons.

Smoke was choking Fargo, and his Ovaro was getting temperamental to handle, so he rode slowly back to the post.

Marshall intercepted him, highly excited yet dampened by worry. "Get away from there, Fargo! These fools are playing for keeps. We better get back to our wagons or maybe we'll get a dose of the same."

It was Fargo's idea, too. He could no nothing here. Nobody could help, so fast was the wind-driven flame eating out the vitals of the camp. He led the way and Marshall rode at his flank, twisting in the saddle to look back. For once in his life, the garrulous wagon master was too impressed by the works of another to find the words that normally spouted so readily from his lips.

Fargo chose a good stiff pace, watching the shadows along the trail for the first hint of danger. Then a long, barreling roar from behind drew his glance back. And there, like a bloody finger against the black backdrop, was the crowning mark of Mormon renegade venom.

At a dozen places within Fort Bridger, hungry tongues of fire laved high against the velvet sky. And even as Fargo looked, these united into a horrendous pillar of fire. Now nothing could save the old post that had stood guard against hostile tribesmen, that had been the rendezvous of the fur-laden mountaineers and free trappers, that had served the milling hordes of emigrants moving westward like a locust horde in late '40s through the '50s.

There was something tragic about this that caught strongly at Fargo's throat, bidding him turn about and return to do what little he could to fight the holocaust. He set his mind stoutly against the thought, as he had against the visceral urge to save Rachel, squared himself in the saddle, and took a faster pace eastward.

The Kentucky wagon train drowsed under the stars, some miles ahead. In it were peacefully sleeping women and children, and men to whom war was just a word.

7

Rounding the point that hid them from Fort Bridger, Fargo and Hap Marshall held their mounts to long lopes. As the post dropped far behind, they eased into a more sustainable pace, but continued watching the trail with critical eyes.

Tension remained high when they arrived back at camp. The settlers, already worried by their long absence and smelling the smoke wafting on night breezes, bombarded Marshall and Fargo with questions.

They responded with a brief account of the fort's destruction, relating just enough to stimulate vigilance without arousing undue fear, and then turned in.

Fargo lay awake for quite some time. When the camp had quieted and he was sure he wouldn't be noticed, he stoked up his cook fire embers to better see by, and checked the money belt, pouch by pouch. The contents were thick rolls of greenbacks, more than two hundred thousand dollars when he'd counted it all out. Stamped on the front of the belt, dimly discernible through the sweat stains that corroded the leather, was the three-rung ladder brand of Jophiel Ladderer. For quite some time after that, too, Fargo lay awake pondering.

The night passed without further alarm, yet Fargo greeted the sun with less peace of mind than if there had been an attack.

With a rifle guard ready on the box of each wagon, the train rolled into the trail, taking a leisurely and wary course toward Fort Bridger. It was only a half day's journey, and a sorry sight greeted the settlers when they rounded the point of the hills about noon. The fort was a smoldering pile of ash. The twin lines of ruin, once army tents and wagons, were fire-blackened earth. Standing alone was the Mormon post, around it soldiers erecting brush shelters, and cooks puttering around their big, smoking cook fires. Across the creek on lush grass, army horses and mules grazed under guard, part of the stampeded herd.

A quarter-mile upcreek, Fargo supervised the circling of the wagons. When it was done and fuel had been gathered, animals driven onto feed, and fires built, Fargo walked down to the Mormon post, jammed now with troopers and civilians in tight little knots, arguing excitedly. Barred from entering by a sentry, he was told there was nothing for sale, all supplies having been commandeered by the army. That was not what Fargo was after, so he hung around awhile, conversing and eavesdropping.

When he returned to the wagons, he had a better grasp of the situation. Several men had been shot, one slain, and numbers were nursing bad burns, acquired in the destruction of the old fort by flame. After the fire, the army had taken over the Mormon post for headquarters and had discovered that Magee and Wayland had vanished, evidently fleeing from potential arrest. Come dawn, a commission of Mormons had shown up for a powwow that was still going on, though it appeared they were cooperating to preserve order, joining their militia to the army command, sending tents and supplies, and so forth. The Phalanx of Gideon had failed, if their intent had been to provoke a confrontation. On the other hand, nobody knew where to collar this secret sect of renegades. So Fargo would still be leading the settlers into danger, but now not quite as blindly.

The wagons rolled southwestward, Fargo stretching them along the trail until exhaustion of the teams forced outspanning long past sunset. Where the branches of Black's Creek join flows at the foot of the Quintas, a circle was made. While fuel was being gathered and the animals moved out to graze, Fargo drew Marshall aside, his eyes fixed upon the mountains.

"We might be attacked tonight, Hap."

"I kinda think these renegades might pass us, havin' bigger fish to fry while they got the military hamstrung. You got a particular reason?"

Two hundred thousand of them, Fargo thought, though he said nothing about the money belt. "Why would they give us a break? After tomorrow we'll be down out of the hills and out of their range."

"Not worth ignorin', I'll grant. What have you in mind?"

"I'll sit tight on that mesa, get on the tail of any visitors swinging in for the herd. You stick a dozen men armed with pistols and repeaters with the stock, ready to run them for the circle at first hint of trouble. Anybody trying to stop it would have to cut across the fire from the wagons. That way we could work less on saving stock and more on killing raiders."

Fargo's plan was repeated during the dinner hour, when Marshall chose his dozen men—stout, fearless settlers proven in the mire of the Overland Trail. In the aftermath of dusk, the purple Quintas Mountains were turning inky black. Fargo snatched a pickup from Hap's tailgate grub box, visited the posted riflemen, and stepped from the circle. Moments later he was ahorse, skirting the train toward the mesa.

He had traveled perhaps half of the distance when, on pausing to check his bearings, he glimpsed the dark form of a man riding behind him. The man rode as if following Fargo, studying the growth on either side, hesitating from time to time to peer and listen. Quietly Fargo eased his horse into a shouldering fringe of huckleberry and saplings until he was concealed, then waited, senses acute.

Presently came the click of hooves, and through the foliage he watched the man's approach. Another moment, and Fargo cussed irritably under his breath, recognizing the rider was no man at all, but Elaine Talbot dressed in her late husband's workpants and shirt. He remained hidden while the young widow paused to glance about, then came on by slowly, apparently satisfied. Not until Elaine was past him did Fargo call to her, a note of exasperation in his voice.

"You're on the right track, Elaine."

She jerked, startled, and whirled in her saddle, gasping as Fargo emerged from the brush. "Oh! You about gave me a conniption."

"What brings you by?"

"Why, nothing in particular. I was simply on my regular constitutional for the horse, the way you advised," she replied. She jigged the animal back beside Fargo and eyed him from under long lashes that veiled, but did not hide, the challenge in her glance. "What a pleasant surprise, running into you."

"Yeah, great. Tonight's far too risky for you to have left camp."

"It is? But you'll escort me safely back to camp, won't you?"

"I'm not returning to camp now, perhaps not till morning." He motioned toward the mesa. "I'm heading up there and watching for a sneak attack."

"Well, if it's that perilous, I mustn't ride alone." She spurred her horse on toward the mesa, calling back, "Besides four eyes are better than two."

Fargo struck after her, muttering. Elaine Talbot

seemed proper and respectable, as if she should be playing organ at some church, but it occurred to him that she may well be more dangerous than her daughter—much more dangerous than any man.

Soon they began to climb the sloping hillside. Elaine rode alongside Fargo now, and with seeming inadvertence, her horse kept dancing sideways, bumping foreshoulders with his Ovaro. Fargo also grew aware that her knee nudged his thigh and that she rode closer than was absolutely necessary, swaying toward him and smiling faintly in her tantalizing manner.

The ascent steepened and grew more rugged, and from midway on up, the unmarked route was lost in darkness. Just short of the rim, they reached a ledge that overlooked an expanse of terrain below, including the wagon train. The view was not as wide as an all-round vista from the crest, but the ledge split like a notch through the mesa, with no apparent path to the top. Fargo tried nonetheless, dismounting by some nearby growth to search for some way that might lead them up. Elaine sat slim and straight in her saddle, watching him, her eyes shadowed and unreadable. Her mare ambled over and nuzzled his pinto. Then both horses put their heads down and began to graze.

"The notch's like a fault line, a natural cutback into the hill chain behind the mesa. But no way up short of wings," Fargo informed her as he returned, shaking his head. "This is as far as we can go."

"A shame. I'd have liked to go all the way with you."

They did not speak for a minute, just stared at each other. Fargo could not judge her comment by the expression of her shaded eyes, but he was very aware of the pattern of her breasts under her shirt and the snug fit of her denims over her hips.

Elaine broke their stare. She swung a leg lithely over her saddle cantle and stepped down.

"What do you think of me, Skye?"

"What do you mean?"

"You think I'm shameless. Wanton."

"That's not true."

She was so close he could feel her warm breath and smell her lilac-scented soap. "What else can you think of me, flirting this way?"

"That you're restless and lonely."

"Bored." She sighed. "Ever dutiful, ever reasonable, ever so virtuous, while my giddy daughter enjoys life. She'll be fifty years old before she has a lick of sense, if she has any then. If I'd had less sense at the time, I wouldn't have married Sam when I was seventeen, but I was being logical and Sam was always practical. A good provider, too. I haven't had it bad, just dull."

"And that's why you were heading west?"

"That's why. Something new, fresh, to get us out of our rut. Instead, Sam is in a hole, and out West a widow's lot is drudgery." She placed a hand on his arm. "But not now. You don't expect a sneak attack yet, do you?"

"If I knew when to expect it, Elaine, it wouldn't be a sneak attack. But yes, it's probably too early, and they'll wait till the camp is bedded asleep." He strolled with her toward the rim. "I still need to keep a lookout, just in case, and that's awful boresome."

"Sure, we can watch while you're boring and I'm bored. Why not?"

Reaching out, Fargo grabbed her by the arms. He was impulsive and rough as he pulled her toward him, bruising his mouth down on hers. He could feel her tense and resist. Good, he told himself, she will break away, and that will be the end of it.

In the midst of this conviction, Fargo felt fire come into her mouth. Her arms went around him and amazed him with the strength and greed of their embrace. Her hand rose and the nails dug into the back of his neck. And when finally she took her lips from his, she did not pull away but pressed, rubbing against him, her head thrown back a little, mouth parted, eyes shiny.

"Now that," she whispered huskily, "is more like it."

Fargo felt her undulations through his taut loins. Well, why not? She wanted it, and what better way to pass time, where there still was time? He unknotted her kerchief and drew it from around her neck. Breathing audibly, she plucked it from him and tossed it aside, then began removing her shirt, bunching it loosely, and shrugging it over her head. Fargo followed suit, shucking his buckskins and hiding the money belt in the folds, while she discarded her boots, jeans, and chemise, baring her large-areolaed breasts.

On tiptoes, then, she brought her mouth to his, softly, lips tingling at the promised contact, cherishing the promise before the act. Fargo embraced her, his hands on her hips and gliding along the silken stretch of her pantaloons, waiting for her to make the next move. She did. Deftly unbuckling his belt and popping the buttons of his fly, she tugged down his pants, slowly, her hand inching over his thighs to free his burgeoning erection.

Now Fargo moved to do the same to the string of her pantaloons, opening them and lowering them just to the very point where the cleft between her legs began to show. He leaned back deliberately and eyed her curly thatch, a more luxuriant growth than her daughter's. She stroked his rigid shaft gently, rubbing its crown. Together they finished undressing each other, momentarily standing naked while they scanned the landscape and then their own naked bodies, before slipping down on the mattress of their garments.

His fingers slid gently up the inside of her legs. He stroked her loins while he bent and kissed each nipple, her shoulders, the smooth line of her throat. Then, moaning with deep animal purrings, Elaine pushed him on his back to receive her erotic fondlings. She shifted to kiss him again and give him her tongue, sighing with pleasure.

Fargo felt her tremble, felt her weight, and enjoyed her ardent advances as she kissed his neck and ears and his tiny nipples. Her mouth laved fire on his chest, then teased lower, moving past the navel and dipping to his inner thighs. And when the tension was unbearable, she went down on him, trying to swallow all of his girth. Fargo stiffened, tensing his muscles. She dug her hands under his hips and encouraged his motions, taking as much as she could. Her tongue was rough, taunting his sensitivity. Then she took the length of him and slid back again his entire length to repeat, and repeat again, her lips clasping him in a tightly milking oval.

"You . . . better be ready," Fargo panted in warning.

Elaine laughed. She climbed atop Fargo, undulating as she lowered herself, slowly enveloping his rigid shaft until she squatted, pressing against him. Fargo gasped as she impaled herself and was reminded of how tight her daughter had been. She hovered above him, thrusting with her hip and buttock muscles, pumping his hardness as fast as she could, pummeling Fargo against their clothes wadded beneath him. Fargo responded with a quickening tempo of pistoning surges to match her frenzied rhythm, sucking one swaying breast into his mouth, flicking her distended nipple with his tongue, and fondling her other breast with his hand.

Her desire continued building to an insane pitch. She writhed and squirmed in a dozen directions. Fargo felt his excitement mounting higher and sensed he was on the brink of release. The tang of her sweat was on his tongue; her dilated gaze glowed with ecstasy as, together, they hammered at yet a faster pace, pushing deeper, their naked bodies slapping and rubbing tempestuously.

Elaine tried to say something, but she could no longer speak. She moaned, shivering from the electric impact of her orgasm while the hot jets of Fargo's bursting climax flooded deep up inside her belly. He pulled her tighter to his pulsing groin as they seemingly merged flesh and bone. Then he sagged, exhausted and drained. Elaine slumped over him, stretching her legs back so she could lie with him clamped inside her, their bodies entwined as they gazed out over the ledge for signs of attackers below, spotting nothing.

Finally, almost drowsily, she said, "Uh-oh," and reluctantly slid off him. "I have to piddle," she explained demurely, and she flitted off behind one of the boulders.

Fargo lay surveying the view in a contented stupor. Then abruptly there came to his ears another sound, farther away in the direction of the notch—a faint clicking noise like that made by the heat of horses' irons on stony ground.

Scrambling up, he padded naked back into the notch and glanced up at the dark bulk of the hills. The night did not seem quite so black now, moonglow and starlight enabling him to scan the outlines of the rocky terrain. For a long moment there were no more betraying sounds, but when they came—the slight jinglings of metal against metal—he felt sure they came from the suspected fault-line cut beyond the notch.

He squatted motionless, peering up at the dark hillsides. The beat of irons grew louder. Topping a distant ridge that swelled upward from a deep hollow, he perceived a line of horsemen appearing in a constant stream against the murky night sky. Fifty, at least.

Maybe seventy-five. A hundred at most. Two abreast, maybe three; it was hard to determine.

Elaine came to him, shamelessly nude, her eyes dreamy and half-closed, her flesh still hot to the touch. She hunkered beside him, curling against his shoulder.

"Shh," he cautioned, and pointed at the riders.

She pressed tighter, catching sight of the mysterious group flowing by. There was something furtive and purposeful about these slow-pacing horsemen. After another moment, the last of the string filed past and the low thunder of their passage was fading.

"What are they up to?" Elaine asked in a hushed voice.

"Up to no good," Fargo replied softly. "Let's trail them."

Returning to their well-flattened pile of clothes, they swiftly sorted garments and dressed, then checked rigging, tightened cinches, and remounted. As an afterthought, Elaine dug into one of her saddlebags and brought out a Colt .31 baby dragoon pistol, which for quick convenience she tucked in the waistband of her jeans.

They jigged their horses back through the notch toward the hogback where they'd spied the riders. It was a hard scramble over the broken ground, and once there, they paused to get their bearings before following the back-hill trail up the passage. They tried to keep their own noise to an absolute minimum.

For quite a time the riders remained invisible, lost in the night and distance ahead as they traveled the hollows and ridges, skirted banks, and curved among a series of gaps and tables. Eventually the stretch of hills began petering out. Fargo and Elaine negotiated a steep slope and were just poking their heads over the crest when Fargo motioned to veer slightly so that they topped the slope where a bristle of growth cast a deep gloom. The other side was jagged, rubbled terrain where only renegades and predators would care to tread. Almost at the bottom, the riders were pouring from a slender bench along a route that twisted among scrub and stone in the direction of the wagon camp.

"Looks like they're aiming to attack," Elaine said fretfully, and touched her pistol. "Shall I shoot to warn the train?"

Fargo shrugged. "At this range, you'll just warn the attackers."

"Yes, and they may hit back with rifles. I don't care for those odds." She started her horse down the slope, adding grimly, "Even if they scattered, they'd only regroup and try some other night."

"Yeah, and if we wait too long, they can do the train plenty of damage. In love and war, timing is everything . . ."

Well before they reached level ground, they could hear the riders galloping toward the circled wagons. They lashed their horses in fast pursuit, favoring the brush and pools of shadows so they would not be spotted by any of the horsemen who might glance behind. Then, when the black outline of the wagons took shape, their dingy white covers etched in moonglow, Fargo and Elaine lined out, horses under free rein and to hell with sightings. In the east there was the pale, dawnlike hint of a moon. Against this, almost as if they had sprung from the ground, was suddenly silhouetted the surging mass of riders.

"Oh, God! We're too late, too late," Elaine cried frantically.

"Get hold of yourself!" Riding aslant, his hat brim pressed back as he split the breeze, Fargo shouldered his Sharps, his eyes straining through the gloom ahead. "Fire now! One shot, save the others! Shoot once, now!"

Sweeping up her pocket pistol, Elaine blasted every

round skyward. "This is a fight! Wake up! Wake and fight!"

Deafening her screaming plea was the thunderous rifle shot Fargo cannoned into the throng ahead. A rider somersaulted off the back of his saddle, discombobulating others with the sudden scare of a counterattack from their rear. Its shattering blast and the firing of that pistol startled the settlers to rousing alert, and within thirty seconds after the alarm, an inferno was loose in Utah Territory. After the hushed strain of waiting, the tension of guarding, the settlers were ready. The drumming of hoofbeats, the raiders' yells, the cusses of settler men, their wives screeching and their children wailing, rose like the voices of countless souls lost in hell.

Elaine's horse caromed off that of a raider, spilling it. From the ground, the fallen rider sent lead at her. Fargo triggered his revolver, saw the man flatten; then, shifting, he fired again. A charging rider toppled, his ghastly white face, terribly contorted, a black hole between his eyes. Elaine drove her panicked mare on toward the wagons, defenseless, her only weapon empty.

Fargo rode close behind, trying to protect her, realizing their peril from the settlers' blind-shooting fury. Every wagon was a smoking fort, from which the sounds of gunfire rolled as families defended their stakes like devils. Their bullets raked into the running lines of riders sweeping around and between them.

Fargo felt a stinging across his left shoulder, but was too fighting mad to care. Through the ruck of plunging riders, he glimpsed Elaine reach the makeshift barricade between two chained wagons. Her horse jumped the hastily assembled wall of kegs and crates. He reined about and headed toward the stock pasture, crossing bloodied ground littered with the still forms of men and of horses that squealed their agony. He had not gone far when he caught a glimpse of the

Gideonite renegade who'd grilled him in the smithy shack. The man was among a group of riders galloping to join a larger force.

Fargo veered in pursuit, while guns from the wagon circle drove the renegades back, whittling them down. They faltered as a group, the compact target they made breaking apart, scattering individually. Nearing, Fargo could hear his target exhorting everyone within shouting range, his hate-mongering yells inflaming those who remembered Haun's Mill, Carthage Jail, and Nauvoo. There were also those who looked at him in disgust or as if he were balmy, hombres of a breed Fargo recognized from many places, many times, including the Mormon post last night—vicious, gun-heavy lobos tight of mouth and long on twist, earning their keep by cruelty and violence.

He lined in on that voice, scanning quickly from wagons to herd. The dozen riflemen Marshall had picked were rolling the right raider flank, each apparently determined to do his part until he died. The settlers responsible for the herd were losing some stock, but already they had moved most of the cattle into the corral of wagons, from whence the settlers defending the train were pouring lead into the renegade ranks. The confused and desperate battle still could go either way, but it was scarcely the surprise party cakewalk the attackers had anticipated.

Satisfied, Fargo concentrated on his man, less than a hundred yards away. Suddenly aware of the onrushing threat, the man pivoted, obviously astonished. He leveled his revolver, and his slugs zipped about Fargo as he came in. Failing to down the Trailsman, the man spun on his horse and spurred down an embankment, the rising hiding him instantly, leaving Fargo to make a choice. Which way would the man break?

Guessing the Gideonite would rein toward the fight at the circled wagons, Fargo rode to cut him off. The battle, he noticed, seemed to be tilting in their favor, the settlers cozied in behind cover while those attacking suffered mounting casualties. Even the most fanatic must have soon realized that they stood a good chance of dashing to their death.

When again Fargo glimpsed him, his prey was racing toward the watercourse willows, having gained another hundred yards. Fargo gave chase, scorning the bullets sent winging back at him. Still holding his fire, he saw three raiders break from the scrub, and heard the man's wild yell of relief as they turned, shooting. Fargo neck-reined his Ovaro, slewing for the willows, shooting at the riders as they were sifting to cut him off. He saw gun flashes licking from the timber, heard a raider howl as he tumbled from his horse.

The Ovaro blundered, the willow break too thick and tall to be mowed through readily. Aware he made a dandy target sitting aboard his stymied horse, Fargo leapt down and rolled into the willows, rising to his knees. Crackling brush heralded a charging enemy on horseback, coming in behind the Ovaro and momentarily stuck.

Fargo sprang up and aside as he fired. The rider gasped a curse, quit the saddle, hurled himself forward, triggering. Fargo fired again, heard life quit his opponent, then was borne down and pinned by the corpse. His brain clicked. "I got that damned Fargo," he shouted hoarsely.

"Good!" That was the man, that questionable leader. "Fetch the money belt and you get a nice piece of it."

Fargo heard the man approaching. Hurriedly he freed himself from the deadweight, snatching up the rider's fallen pistol as a backup for his almost empty revolver. The man came wedging through the willows. "Where is he, Seth?"

"Here," Fargo growled, aimed, and fired. And missed.

The man staggered back, his short pistol answering with spaced thunder. Fargo dropped to one knee and took deliberate aim, ignoring the wild slugs around him. This shot drew a rattly scream from the man, who sat plunk down, mouthing curses, his gun barrel weaving circles as he strove desperately to focus on his target.

Fargo triggered once more; the hammer clicked. Bracing himself for the shock of a bullet, Fargo traded his empty Colt for the dead rider's weapon, an abused, crack-gripped Starr .44 that could as easily blow up his face as spit out a slug. But his opponent couldn't drive his flagging senses. He and Fargo fired at virtually the same instant. The man's bullet kicked dirt into Fargo's face. Fargo's desperate shot winged true and hard. The man gave a rattling cough, a final sullen flare lit his eyes, then he collapsed forward into the willow litter and lay still and shapeless against the earth.

Fargo stood up, breathing harshly. He could hear his Ovaro moving around in the brush and started toward it, then heard something else—the trompings of hooves, thrashings of brush, muttering gruff voices. He paused, aware the noises were closing in too fast, here too soon for him to be able to load his percussion revolver. He only had time to glance dubiously at the Starr—

Then the remaining pair of horsemen were upon Fargo, pistols ready.

8

The two riders plunged afile from the willows and half-reined down where moonlight slanted through branches to dapple the bodies of their confederates. Swearing unpiously, eyes questing through the moon shadows, they glimpsed Fargo standing close by and swung to train their cocked pistols.

"Your cronies had their chance," Fargo stated, cold and hard. "They lost their marbles. You'd be smart to let them lie and get out while you can."

"Murderin' mobocrat!" the first man raged, jumping his mount ahead with digging rowels, firing at point-blank range. His partner came spurring right smack behind, revolver blasting dead-set on Fargo.

The lead horse barged into the clumped, intertwined willows and lurched awry, the horse behind butting into it. The jostling upset the aim of the riders, their bullets sizzling close but not drawing blood. Fargo, gun barrel already tilted, had but to squeeze the trigger of the double-action Starr twice. The riders hurtled from their saddles, dead before they hit ground.

Trudging to his horse, Fargo loaded and capped his own Colt, then tossed the Starr over by its dead owner, adding a silent word of thanks as he mounted. With three other horses under hoof, it took some effort to extricate the Ovaro, but at last they cleared the willows. Breathing gunsmoke for air, weary and worn, he headed upbank for the wagon camp, which was screened from view by a bordering copse of trees and underbrush.

The raid had ended, suddenly but not surprisingly; attacks, once blunted, usually folded fast. In the distance, surviving raiders were under gun of pursuing settlers as they fled southeastward—little packs of them cut to ribbons and racing for the badlands.

Leveling off from the slope, Fargo let the pinto seek its own relaxed pace as they neared the camp, which was around the end of the corpse ahead. Lulled by his nearness to the camp and the calm, he neglected to keep watch on the Ovaro's ears, else he would have been forewarned. Instead, he kept on unawares, and was following a shortcut through a crop of low willows when his horse shied violently. The click of a cocking rifle ran ominously through the night stillness. Almost unseated, Fargo righted himself and went to the withers, drawing his pistol as flame lanced from the shadows and lead scorched the buckskin fringe across his back.

Fargo, his horse gathering into a swift run, turned in the saddle and fired back across the cantle. He shot at the muzzle flash, shot twice more. He saw the figure of a man stumble from cover and go down, lift himself to his knees, and send two more shots through the willows. Bullets hummed past Fargo, buzzing like hornets. He loosed two more shots and then his straining mount bore him along the path, out of the copse and onto the flat where the train was ringed in a tight circle.

Gunfire blazed from the circle of tops, and Fargo, under dangerous fire from his own side, waved and yelled his name. The shooting ceased and settlers came running toward him, apologizing for the closeness of their fatal error and blaming it on overwrought nerves.

Marshall and perhaps half the men had gone out chasing the raiders, leaving these others fearing that some new attack would catch them understrength. They fretted that the ambusher was a spy, and Fargo led them back into the trees to snoop about, knowing as he did so that it was a wasted effort. Whoever that was wouldn't wait around to sample the fury of the wagon men. Strained tempers cooled as the night failed to give up the bushwhacker, or any sign of him. Everyone went back to the train, where the eventual return of Marshall and party caused another whirlwind of questions and speculations.

When things began to settle down once again and Fargo was preparing to make a round of inspection, a voice spoke his name.

It was Julia, her face a pale blob in the night. Fargo went to her, found her hands cold and her slender body trembling. "What is it, Julia? There's nothing to be feared too much, if we don't get careless. Why, you're crying."

She struggled against her tears, drawing her sleeve across her face. "It's—it's Abel Rasmussen, Skye."

"Bothering you?"

"Oh, no, no, Skye. He's badly hurt. His father's hopelessly drunk, so Mom and I moved him to our wagon, and we've bound his wound as best we can, but I fear he's going to die, and I . . ." She gave a sob. "I don't want him to die."

"Oh-oh." Fargo knew now that his hunch had been right about who had shot at him on his return. The insanely jealous Abel had sneaked from the train and bushwhacked him, which somehow didn't surprise him, though Julia's weepy anguish did. "Sounds like you're a little fond of the big plowboy, eh?"

She nodded, snuffling back her tears. "He likes me, too, I d-don't know why. I want to be nice, but when he's nice, something devilish takes hold of me and I treat him atrociously. I tell him horrid things, like I haven't decided yet whether to accept your proposal. Even when I know you'd never have me, er, in that way. That was last time, and poor Abel looked crushed when he left me. Do you think he—he may have shot himself?"

"Why, of course not. He blundered outside and ran afoul of some renegade who'd come back to catch us napping," Fargo lied cheerily.

With Julia comforted and running alongside, he hurried to her wagon. Elaine cast him a knowing look and indicated Rasmussen squirming on a blanket in the wagon bed, stifling moans of pain. After Elaine had lighted a dip, Fargo examined Abel. A bullet had punctured his side at a glancing angle, drilling along his rib cage for eight, nine inches and emerging clean, leaving a painful flesh wound and two open sores, but no major damage or busted bones so far as Fargo could determine. Rasmussen would suffer a deserved amount of hurt and inconvenience, but would recover completely within a short time.

Rasmussen was conscious but too mortified to look Fargo in the eye, except once when Fargo first began to check him, and he stared pleadfully, fearing retribution. Fargo replaced Elaine's bandage and turned to smile reassuringly at Julia. "Nothing but an underskin poke, girl. You couldn't kill this big buffalo with any one shot. Keep him here tonight, change his dressing tomorrow, spoon your mother's cooking into him, and send him out to work. He's a good man and we'll be needing the likes of him."

With a doleful groan, Rasmussen glanced sheepishly at Fargo. "I'm none o' that, I'm a sidewinderin' skunk. If you done right, you'd take your gun and blow my brains clean out. 'Twas me that— "

"That was more brave than smart, patrolling alone too far afield," Fargo cut in sternly. "You're lucky you're not buzzard bait out there, instead of sparking just about the nicest nurse on these prairies."

Rasmussen caught his wrist, protesting. "You don't

understand. I got to thinking you were taking Julia from me, worrying you were taking advantage of her, or maybe even thinking of marrying her, so I—"

"You grew jealous," Fargo interrupted again, "hotheaded, saying things you didn't really mean. You had to let off some steam. I understand. Me take away your gal? Can't be done, Abel, she's set on you. Now, go to sleep and let that hurt heal some. Good night." He snuffed the candle and left the wagon.

Elaine caught up and accompanied him, silent until they were out of earshot. "Thank you, Skye."

"Not yet. I'm no sawbones, and may have missed some serious stuff."

"You didn't miss forgiving. He attempted to kill you and you know it."

Fargo chuckled. "Whatever gave you such a notion?"

"Abel. When Julia went to fetch you, he panicked, told me what he'd done. He had a fit at seeing you bring me back here today through the fighting. He thought it was Julia. He'd tried to ambush you and you shot him, not knowing who the sniper was. But once you saw him, he knew you'd know, and if you didn't throttle him on the spot—which you didn't— you'd be justified in having him tried and hung." Elaine touched his arm appreciatively. "Enough deaths for one day, right? Including, strange to say, some of Olin Karnes' wagon crew."

Fargo stared at her. "You sure?"

"Oh, yes. The men who stranded us are burned in my memory, unforgettable. I'll point them out to you, come daylight, if you want. On the whole, they're scuffier and not as, well, religious-looking as most of the others."

"They trust to guns, not gods," Fargo replied. "Karnes among them?"

Elaine shook her head. "Thank you again, Skye. Abel isn't bad and Julia will tame whatever hellishness there is out of them both." She caught him in a fierce grip, raised to tiptoe, and kissed his lips. Fargo naturally returned the caress. For a long moment she clung to him, then broke their embrace and, with a parting smile, hurried toward her wagon.

Fargo, brushing his lips with his fingers and gazing after her, heaved a sigh of relief. Then he headed for Marshall's wagon.

Hap was sitting at his cook fire, cross-legged and bare-chested, salving his aches and cramps with horse liniment, while dosing his innards with barrel whiskey. At times the applications appeared to get switched, Fargo noticed as he approached, though Marshall didn't seem to suffer or even to notice.

"If it weren't for all those females sashaying about," Marshall declared when Fargo hunkered alongside, "I'd peel out of my pants. Got a stiff leg I'd hurt while busting a bronc years ago."

"Uh-huh. Well, those old war wounds can be touchy, Hap, and you ought to ease off awhile. Come to consider, the whole train should rest up. Say, a four-, five-day layover," Fargo suggested. "I expect to be back by then."

"Forget it! You're stayin' with us, and we're rollin' on."

"Hap, we've had to drive the train hard. It paid off, but it also costs. Folks are bone-weary, more careless, apt to get hurt. Over thirty are hurting now from wounds, and the faster they can recover, the better. The stock and wagons need care, too, if they're to last. Just look at your own wagon. Patched, tattered, canvas drooped over the bows, like the ribs of your teams. You're boss, Hap, but believe me, you either make an easy maintenance stop here, or face a hard breakdown ahead, a series of them in the middle of nowhere."

Marshall glowered and grumbled, but acquiesced.

"One other thing, Hap, before I go—"

"Save it, 'cause you ain't goin'!"

"Put the camp on full alert. Double watches, keep the herd closer, all those measures. And make sure everyone knows what to do in case of attack."

"Attack? What do you fancy is gonna attack us?"

"More of the same gang that attacked earlier," Fargo said, frowning. "They could strike most anyplace, most anytime. Your guess where is as good as mine. I can't make any sense of who or what they are, either."

An hour later, Fargo rode out of camp. He was packed light for speed, and to help sustain a rapid pace, he brought along a second horse for alternate riding. A sturdy blue roan, it was on loan from Abel Rasmussen, who wouldn't be up to mounting more than Julia for some days yet.

Once clear of the wagon camp, Fargo struck overland in a southeasterly direction. He kept on course—or as much as the jagged landscape would allow—and he kept on horse, maintaining a steady lope that covered the miles without overtaxing his increasingly frazzled mounts, hoping he'd reckoned rightly and would eventually wind up in the vicinity of Blockade Valley.

Blockade Valley, Fargo recalled Wayland claiming, was solely owned by Jophiel Ladderer. Ladderer was also a Mormon deacon, Fargo knew. And if he were to believe that flat-laughing ambusher, he was the father of Rachel.

Two hundred thousand bucks, stuffed in a money belt that wore the Ladderer brand . . . a girl disguised as a boy, hiking cross-country, hiding out in wilderness, horse-swiping, balking at talking or trusting . . . It added up to Rachel being a thief. She must have stolen that money from her father and fled Blockade Valley, sneaking across the Green River, and making a run for it. For all her secrecy and skulking, she must have messed up royally along the line, because she'd been caught and she'd been chased by a swarm of zealots, renegades, common gun thugs, sly yellow dogs like Wayland and Magee, and a meaner breed called Olin Karnes, all slavering in hot pursuit of her . . . for as long as she had the belt.

Now they were hunting him, storming the wagons and no doubt massing to attack again, willing to slaughter every settler to get at him. If they held to habit, though, they'd leave off soon as word spread that he no longer wore the belt. Before they massacred the train, he hoped, he'd be inside Blockade Valley and confronting Jophiel Ladderer. Perhaps his hoyden daughter, too, if she wasn't already condemned and executed. By giving the belt to him, an outsider, he suspected she'd dug her grave deep. Pinching the money was grand larceny in or out of Blockade Valley, but cahooting with a Gentile surely fell under capital offenses as, say, a transgressified malfeasance or an unregenerative atrocity. So it might not do her much good to make restitution, but Fargo would make sure she'd have the money to do it.

Fargo crossed the Green River near Emigrant Springs, far south of the wagon ford. It had begun to rain, but not hard enough or long enough to cause a flooding turmoil like before, but the banks were steep and the current was white-water brutal. Fargo followed the bank downriver some distance, coming eventually to a stretch where the banks dipped in a rounded slope. Less compressed here, the Green appeared to be slightly wider and calmer, yet its foamy rush was still sufficient to cause anyone to approach it with great care.

"Well, let's get this over with," he muttered.

The horses prancing, he kept firm rein and kneed forward, forcing his reluctant mounts to wade in up to the hocks in chilly water. Urged on, the horses struggled across—their hooves fighting the slippery sharp rocks, legs resisting the churning tide. They passed up the east bank and, before proceeding, stood huffing and shivering for a recouperative moment. Then southeastward he headed once again, bearing for Blockade Valley.

"You beller too loud," Magee had told his partner Wayland.

But Wayland had told no more than one of the many versions of Blockade Valley. And Rachel had left out much that Skye Fargo already knew. Mostly he'd heard it firsthand from Jim Bridger, after Bridger returned from guiding that military foray against the Mormons in '57.

On the basis of unsubstantiated news of treasonable behavior in Utah, President Buchanan had replaced Brigham Young as governor with Alfred Cumming of Georgia, and ordered twenty-five hundred troops under Colonel Johnston to "quell the rebellion." Naturally the Mormons resisted, and lost. Johnston made general for crushing all hint of revolt—however, his troops had to remain at Camp Floyd, west of Utah Lake.

Resentment and enmity seethed deep within the Mormon community. Fanatics and hotbloods longed to strike back while plain old outlaws pleaded persecution to excuse their banditry.

As Bridger told it, most tragic were the well-respected Mormons, such as Ladderer, who were forced into exile over the religious principal of "plural marriage." The invading U.S. government decreed that a man should have but one wife. In the eyes of Jophiel Ladderer, and according to his faith, those women were his wives in the eyes of God, to be honored, not cast aside and shamed, their offspring branded illegitimate. Facing arrest and trial for polygamy, he showed the courage of his convictions. With his followers, their wives, and children, Ladderer and kin had fled eastward almost to the boundary of the territory, which since 1850 had stretched to the Continental Divide.

In the shadow of that curving range called Vermillion Bluffs, they had found a fertile valley and settled down, building cabins and fencing range and farm fields, making a sanctuary out of a wilderness. All Jophiel Ladderer and his followers asked now was to be left alone. "Our valley is closed. The trails have blockades. Let outsiders venture here at their own risk, for any trespasser found past the blockades will pay the extreme penalty. This is our Law."

That was as much as Bridger felt sure about. There were nicer names for the place, but somehow Blockade Valley took a hold and stuck.

Closed it didn't stay for long.

Ugly rumors drifted out of Blockade Valley and scattered across Utah and Arizona cow-country. They varied in many details, but out of their twisted warp and woof ran a single thread like a cord dipped in blood. Invaders came in the dead of night, killing, burning, raping. Who those night riders were, how many of them rode into Blockade Valley, still remained a black, blood-spattered mystery. How many rode out of Blockade Valley furnished food for wild speculations. The blame was laid on that long-defunct secret cadre of armed men, the Danites. The government knew history better than that, yet they seemed content to shift the blame on the Danites and let the thing die. No soldiers were sent to Blockade Valley to investigate. Civil authorities were all too willing, even eager to drop the investigation. Let Jophiel Ladderer bury his dead—if he remained alive. Let Blockade Valley hold its own dark secret.

Fargo waited until nightfall before he entered Blockade Valley, so that he might elude possible guards. Six known trails led into the Mormon demesne. It would take too many men to guard those gaps, so Fargo felt fairly safe. Just the same, he rode with his hand on his revolver and he watched the ears of his Ovaro. The horse could see, hear, smell, and feel danger at night, much quicker than any man.

The weather had been working into a thunderstorm, with lightning spreading in swift wide streaks across the sky. With the first hours of night, black clouds were pushing up over the ragged mountain skyline, and the round moon scudded in behind black thunderheads. The growl of thunder kept getting louder and more ominous, and now and then jagged chain lightning ripped the sky. Fargo hoped he'd picketed the blue roan securely enough in that sheltered pocket a couple of miles back; with the advent of the storm, the roan had gone skittish on him and might spook if given a lead.

By the time Fargo got into the valley proper, there wasn't a star left above him and the night was black with the threat of a downpour. He let his Ovaro follow a rutted wagon trail. Split-rail fence paralleled the road on either side, and when the lightning flared, he saw hay fields and orchards and log cabins and barns. He was nearing the heart of the valley. The fences were in good repair, yet there was a neglected look about the windows of the cabins. But horses grazed in the pastures and the haystacks were fenced. The ranches weren't deserted. Neglected, was all.

But it was not the neglect that bothered Fargo as he rode along the wagon road past the little ranches. It was the absence of human life. A creek lined by giant cottonwoods coursed the length of the valley. A bridge spanned the little river and Fargo rode across and around a bend in the road. And sucked in his breath as he reined his horse to a sudden halt.

He had been looking for human beings, for lights. And there they were. Men on foot. Other men on horseback. All armed. All save the two hatless men who stood in the lantern light, hands tied behind their backs. Each stood beside an open grave and an empty coffin. The place was a cemetery. Wooden headboards marked the graves beyond. Half a dozen lanterns sat on the ground. Men moving past the lanterns cast long, distorted shadows on the graveyard. The approaching storm and the black mountains furnished a grim backdrop for the scene.

Six men with saddle carbines stood facing the two hatless men. And these six men were the firing squad.

A tall man rode into the lantern light on a strawberry roan gelding. When he reined up, a long flash of lightning flared, and in its glare Fargo read the ladder brand on the roan's left shoulders. The rider was young, in his middle twenties. Straw-colored hair showed from under the crown of his stetson. He rode with his weight in his left stirrup and there was a challenge in the tilt of his head and the way he sat his horse.

He sat his roan not ten feet in front of the two men, who stood bareheaded, their hands tied, beside the two open graves and crude pine-board coffins. His voice sounded, flat-toned, through the growl of distant thunder.

"You two men," he said, "were caught sneaking into Blockade Valley. Each trail in is marked with warning signs. You ignored those signs and the blockade points. You have been tried and found guilty of trespassing. The penalty for trespassing is death. Have you anything to say before sentence is executed? Have you any message you want sent out?"

One prisoner was in his late teens. In the lightning glare his skin looked yellow and beaded with sweat. He licked his lips, his pale eyes staring at the firing squad as he tried desperately to stand erect. He was using up the last of his ebbing courage with every second of time he had left. He tried to say something but his jaw slacked and the words would not come.

The other prisoner was in his forties. A week's stubble of wiry black beard covered his heavy jaw. His gray hair was matted down by the hat he no longer wore. Bloodshot black eyes glittered under heavy scowling black brows. He was short and powerfully built and bowlegged. He looked like he might be part Indian.

"You're a snake, Tripp!" His voice was a snarl. "A dirty, black-hearted, double-dealin', murderer. You left the pass open. And I was sucker enough to sneak in. You saw this carrot of a kid meet me and pilot me in. I never seen the kid before. But he looks enough like Jack Ladderer to be his brother."

Thunder and lightning drowned out his words. The lightning struck close. Close enough to spook the roan gelding into jumping. Then the rain came. Huge splattering drops. And the lighting flare that had blinded their eyes was gone, and the darkness was thick and the lanterns glowed dimly.

"Get ready!"

The man on the roan gelding lifted his hat and stood in his stirrups as he rode out of the line of fire. The men of the firing squad shifted saddle carbines they had cuddled in their left arms.

"Take aim!"

The six steel gun barrels were leveled. Six heads tilted as the firing squad lined their gun sights. The youth stiffened. He was using every shred of his courage now—all the guts he had. He clamped his teeth to keep from screaming, his lips moving stiffly like he was whispering a prayer.

Skye Fargo sat his horse like a man in the grip of a nightmare. He wanted to yell out something that would halt this execution. He wanted to take a shot at Tripp on his strawberry roan gelding. The rain splattered on his face, on the hands that gripped the Sharps as he slid it from its scabbard and now held half-raised, pointing at Tripp. And he had to fight back that crazy impulse that would ruin his slim chance here in Blockade Valley.

"Fire!"

9

The six saddle carbines spat fire.

The short swarthy man doubled up, head lobbing forward and his bowed legs, hobbled at the ankles, hinging at the knees. He pitched over onto his face and lay still, bullet-riddled and leaking blood on the ground beside his empty coffin. The boy's legs gave way and he collapsed like a long empty sack beside the pine-board lidless coffin.

The gun echoes blended into the rolling thunder and then faded as rain sluiced down in a sudden torrent. One of the lanterns guttered out.

Swearing loudly, Tripp and his roan moved out of the rain-filled darkness into the light of another lantern. "Throw that damn breed's carcass into its coffin and dump him in his grave." He leaned from his saddle, picked up the lighted lantern, and rode with it over to where the boy lay.

Fargo, dismounting, began to ease off trail before they broke their party and caught him out. The Ovaro stepped lightly, and the brush was spindly enough to allow Fargo to keep watch. Tripp was over where the boy lay, holding the lantern. Suddenly Fargo's breath hitched, his eyes staring at something he thought was a miracle.

The kid was moving. He rolled over on his side and there was no blood on his shirt, and when he lifted his head, his umber-red hair was rain-sodden and his face was contorted, his eyes saucer-wide. He tried to choke back a quaver in his voice, Fargo eyeing his mute struggle while gliding closer, leaving the Ovaro ground-reined behind. For his troubles, the boy managed to catch the hiccups instead.

Tripp leaned over the saddle horn. "Hold your dumb breath. You still got it, but you won't get off this easy next time." He was lowering the lantern close to the boy's pale face, his left hand poking a piece of paper—Fargo couldn't tell precisely what—into the boy's shirt pocket. "You can tell that to Jophiel Ladderer, and to your snooty sister when you give her that. Maybe so it'll learn 'em a lesson."

Now the boy found his voice, shrill and brittle. "Damn you! God damn you to eternal hell, Azrael Tripp!"

Tripp was straightening, and motioned with the lantern. "Turn the little shitface loose, men. Now, get the hell away outta sight before Azrael Tripp forgets how softhearted—"

The rest was drowned out, the storm bursting apart at every seam. A solid sheet of water drenched the lantern in Azrael Tripp's hand, and the lanterns on the ground guttered out. Fargo began sloshing back to his Ovaro, the ground like brown jelly. When the lightning flashed, he could see the Tripp's crew drop the dead man's open pine-board coffin into its grave, and a couple of them were shoveling in the rain-soaked dirt on top of it. Azrael Tripp and most of the others were pulling on yellow slickers and all but the two men with the shovels were mounted.

The boy was mounting a chunky dark hammerhead. Keeping an eye on him, Fargo quickened his pace toward the Ovaro, slipping once and just catching himself before his whole body slapped into the mud. His hands were filthy. The boy was not yet fully seated, but before he was, before he hooked his right stirrup, his hammerhead shot away with a head-tossing, teeth-baring whinny. Some of the crew horses replied shrilly, and Tripp's roan gave a trumpeting peal, but the Ovaro merely swung a disgusted look and a disdainful snort at the departing hammerhead. Unfortunately, Fargo was boosting his leg up just then, with his hands too mud-slicked to gain a firm grip, and when the horse swung around on a sudden impulse, without any warning, Fargo went slinging off. And down. Facedown. With a full-bodied *splat!* that luckily was muffled by a crack of thunder.

Cussing, Fargo reared upright on his feet again, slathered with muck now front and back. Scraping his clothes, slipping over rocks and slithering in the grease-slick mud, he rushed for his horse and sprang aboard, jigging forward through the brush to the wagon road, pausing first to glance around. The boy was riding straight toward Fargo and the bridge he had just crossed. The Trailsman hurried across the bridge in the dark, then pulled off the road in behind heavy brush. When the kid came along, Fargo rode out of the brush and alongside him in the dark.

"Can't you damn renegades let me along?" The boy's voice had a hopeless tone to it.

Fargo said nothing. He hadn't made up his mind exactly what he was going to do, and for a while they rode along in silence, the downpour drenching them. Then Fargo remembered the slicker on his saddle and he twisted around and jerked at the saddle strings, shaking the slicker loose. When the lightning flashed again, he crowded his horse in close and shoved the slicker at the boy.

"Put it on."

Fargo let on not to notice the boy was crying. The boy twisted his head sideways, then straightened and was staring hard at Fargo when the brief lightning flare died. "You ain't one of Tripp's renegades. Who are you?" The voice sounded sharp with suspicion as it came out of the blackness.

"Slicker won't do much good. You're kind of damp. But it'll ward the chill off, and what you just went through leaves a man sort of shocked, and you can catch cold quick that way. Pneumonia's killed more tough men in bed than busted bones ever did. And put on this hat—my head needs washing anyhow."

"Who are you?"

"A hell of a question. Pull on the slicker. We'll argue when we get there."

"Get where?"

"Wherever you're going. Home, isn't it?"

"Listen, stranger, if you think you're trickin' me into leadin' you to the hideout, you're feeble-brained. You better kill me now and be done with it. Or let's ride back and let Azrael Tripp finish what I wish he'd done while he was at it." The boy pulled up in the mud and rain.

The lightning flared again. Fargo ducked and grinned. Bareheaded, he reached out and placed his hat on the boy, but his hat was too big, dropping down over his sodden, reddish-brown hair and over his ears. Fargo's grin widened. "My hat needs a lantern wick inside the sweatband. But right now it's the only hat in stock." He threw the open slicker across the boy's slim shoulders. "Try it on for size. I'm not trying to locate anybody's hideout. But I just saw how Tripp welcomes strangers, and I've got nowhere to go, you might say, but away from his gang. Are you a Ladderer?"

"I'm Matt Ladderer. I've one sister and Deacon Ladderer is our father. We're all that's still alive of the Ladderer family. I'm telling you nothing you don't already know. Now let me alone. Or kill me, I'm not scared to die. He's sent you to try to hoodwink me so I'll lead you to where—"

"When this rain lets up," Fargo cut in, "your horse

will leave a trail in the mud a blind man can pick up and follow. Travel on while the storm will still blot it out. Or before he sets somebody to trail you. And if you can tell me where a stranger in a strange land can hide out for a while, you'd be saving me from that firing squad I just watched. Do me that favor and maybe I'll live long enough to pay you back. From what I've seen and heard, Jophiel Ladderer could do with a little help."

"That half-breed Ponca lied the same lie. He told me he'd slipped into Blockade Valley to side with us against Tripp. Claimed he saw Tripp kill my brother Jack, and as payback, he'd fetch in men to wipe out Tripp and his renegade crew. He almost talked me into taking him to see my father, when some of Tripp's hands rode up on us and made us go to the old meeting house that Tripp turned into a saloon. Ponca and Tripp had a private talk, and I bet Ponca lied his bluest best. Didn't help him none, and won't help you none, either. Quit trying to soften me with a string of worn-out lies!"

"Then here's where our trails fork."

Fargo rode on ahead. He wasn't angry with the kid. Young Matt Ladderer had just been through an ordeal that was grim enough to jangle the nerves of any tough man. He let his horse take its own course, slogging on down the muddy lane in the crashing din of the storm. He did not look back. He did not know the boy was riding close behind him until he had ridden clear of the long lane and the country ahead was open.

"Swing off to the north." Matt caught up with him. "I been thinking. I'd sure hate to make a mistake and let another man get murdered by Azrael Tripp. I'll take you to a hideout. There's plenty places back in the roughs where a man can hole up a long time, then move on to a new place when he gets to know the

111

country better. I'm sure taking a stranger's word for a lot. Did with Ponca, and I know he lied to me."

"It sounded like you were almost talked into taking him to your pa."

"Almost. But when him and Tripp came out from jawing, Tripp told his crew they'd caught a Karnes working as a Magee and Wayland rep. Said he figured it out that Ponca snooped on Magee and Wayland for his relatives, that he was actually another one of the stinkin' Karnes clan. Then Tripp ordered them to take me and the double-dealin' breed to the boneyard and make us dig our own graves."

Fargo let it slide for a moment, then he asked casually, "Who is Karnes?"

"Largest family of cutthroats there ever was, the devil's spawn of Porter Karnes! He was hired on by Azrael Tripp, back when Tripp was looking for likely men for his renegade crew. Not the Azrael Tripp you seen back yonder. His father, Azrael Senior. When my father came to this valley to take refuge, he brought Tripp and his family and a few of their friends along. Tripp repaid us by guiding in the Karnes clan. They were all good at killing, so good that Tripp agreed to a bounty of sorts. For each dead man Porter Karnes brought in, he could take himself another bride from our women." The boy suddenly went silent. "I've talked too much," he muttered.

"Maybe. Maybe not enough. Blockade Valley's got a fascinating history. Who," Fargo then asked, lifting his voice above the storm, "are Magee and Wayland?"

"Don't know," the boy said stiffly.

Fargo knew Matt lied.

They traveled on after that for a while in silence. The trail petered out and Matt led the way into rough country. It was an hour or more later when they reached a little clearing in the brush and scrub pines. The storm had passed and the black sky was breaking up into big clouds. In the moonlight Fargo saw a small log cabin and beyond it a round pole corral.

"This," Matt said, "is as far as you go along with me."

They rode up to the cabin. The door was shut. There was a small window, the glass broken out of the frame. A carbine barrel poked out through the window, and from the darkness inside sounded a brittle voice, "Reach!"

Fargo raised both hands to the level of his wide shoulders. Young Matt rode up behind him and yanked the Trailsman's revolver from its holster. Then he jerked the Sharps free and tossed it on the ground. Fargo found himself looking into the round black hole of his own Colt.

"C'mon out, I got him! 'Cept for his knife," Matt called.

"Let him keep it. I might make him use it later."

The carbine stayed aimed at Fargo while the cabin door opened. A man about thirty stepped outside, six foot one or two, maybe two hundred pounds, with a hardness that didn't come from riding a brass rail. His tousled hair, the shade of dressed harness leather, was brushed under a wide-brimmed, flat-crowned Kansas hat, and he had a big beak of a nose and an anvil for a chin. His range clothes were worn frayed and wet, and in his right hand he held a big old dragoon Colt with its muzzle pointing downward.

"You had us worried, Matt. You were gone too long. Who's he?"

"You ask him, Gabe." Matt pulled off the too-big hat and tossed it to Fargo, grinning. "Thanks for the loan."

"Where's yours?" the man named Gabe asked.

"It fell into my grave." Matt quickly told Gabe how he had met Fargo and fetched him to the cabin for him to look over. Fargo liked the way the boy played down the ordeal of the firing squad, and judged him to be two, maybe three years younger than Rachel.

"He asked about Karnes," Matt said, "and he let on he never heard of Wayland and Magee. But he made me wear his slicker and hat, so I took a chance and brought him here. You're better at sizing folk up than I am, and we can set him afoot here so he can't trail us further."

Gabe walked over to where Fargo sat his horse. "Get down, easy." As Fargo dismounted, he added, "One more renegade." His voice was quiet with contempt. "As if Tripp was shorthanded. Or are you hired out to Magee and Wayland?"

"Not unless they're hiring their own deaths. I've known Magee and Wayland in passing for several years now, and I know them for a pair of thieving hounds."

Matt spoke up, "You know any Karneses? You asked who they was, too."

"And you cleared it up."

"How about clearing up who you are and where you're from," Gabe advised, adding, "We're not the Law here."

"And I'm not on the dodge from the Law," Fargo replied. "I haven't set root anywhere long enough to hail as home, though. Name is Fargo, Skye Fargo."

"Traveling so much, you must've heard the worst of Blockade Valley."

"Well, not the best."

"Then why'd you risk coming here?" the man pressed.

Fargo stared at the rawboned Gabe, realizing he'd been mousetrapped. No lame excuse like wandering in lost would work now; he had to have a strong reason for trespassing, knowing the penalty. He had to think fast, and he figured Gabe was a hard man to lie to. The boy unquestioningly trusted Gabe, and Gabe apparently backed the Ladderers, kid and cause, as though he were a close family friend or loyal retainer. Fargo took a bold chance.

"This is why." Shoving a hand inside his sodden shirt, he unbuckled the money belt and tossed it at Gabe. " 'Less I misread, stamped on the front there is the Ladderer brand. I brought it where it belonged."

Catching the belt in his left hand, Gabe studied the worn brand while Matt watched, engrossed, a strange mixture of eagerness and cold suspicion in both their eyes. Gabe unfastened one of the bulging pouches, and as he drew out a fat roll of currency, Fargo suggested, "I'd rather you count it, both of you, and then take it to Deacon Ladderer or whoever. It's all there."

"Sure, all that's left." Gabe put the roll back. "I can't check it. I don't know the original amount," he said, closing the pouch. He was still pointing his revolver down, but his trigger finger was twitchy as he stepped up close to Fargo. "How come," he demanded in a stony voice, "you got this belt?"

"You'll have to figure that one out for yourself."

Matt growled, looking ready to jump him, but Gabe gave a curt shake of the head. "Stay clear," he ordered the boy, though his eyes were watching Fargo narrowly. And as Fargo leaned forward a little, hitching his mud-soaked pants, Gabe said through clenched teeth, "All right, Skye Fargo, you and me are gonna have it out." And he swung up the barrel of his dragoon.

Fargo abruptly straightened, head high, the hollow of his throat gouged by the Colt's muzzle. In his right hand, however, he gripped his bowie-style hunting knife, whisked from its sheath with practiced stealth when supposedly leaning to hitch his pants. The tip of its razor-honed blade prodded Gabe in the hollow of his throat. "Don't want to carve you up, pal, unless I have to."

Gabe checked the rash impulse to make a fight of it,

but he didn't crawl either. "I don't hold with deceivers and betrayers of unsullied maidens."

"We can agree on that without argument."

Gabe frowned querulously for a moment, as if he were chewing over something, then broodingly remarked, "In some ways she's a woman. In other ways she's still a child, with a streak of tomboy. I taught her to ride; she has way with horses. But she was always running away, and her mother was always sending me to fetch her back before her father found out she'd run off. I called her the Little Rebel. If you seduced Rachel into stealing that money and running off with you, then shooting is too easy a death for you!"

"I confess I did it alone. I never laid eyes on any little girl named Rachel. I stole that cash. You can hang me slow for it," Fargo mocked.

Gabe stared at Fargo, long and hard, then slowly shook his head. "You are a damned liar, Skye Fargo of no place." The pistol in his hand lowered, and as he shoved it in its open holster, Fargo returned his knife to the sheath. Gabe handed him the money belt then, saying, "You ain't done delivering. I warn you now, Deacon Ladderer is a man of peace, but he's had to kill men. And he won't hesitate to kill you to protect himself and what's left of his family."

Matt held Fargo under gun as Gabe went to the cabin. From the broken window he retrieved the carbine that had been pointing out at Fargo, then he went around and led a saddled horse out from behind some brush. Mounting, Matt kept Fargo's firearms while Gabe nudged in close to Fargo, untying a red checkered bandanna from around his neck.

"We'll lead you to the hideout blindfolded." As Gabe was tying the bandanna, he added, "I could rope your hands behind you, but it'd be awkward riding in the roughs. I'll take your word you won't slip your blindfold."

Matt spoke up, "Don't worry, I'll be riding tag. I'll watch for any tomfoolery."

Gabe slid the bridle reins from the Ovaro before Fargo knew it, and began leading his horse. The going got rougher. They traveled a long way in water and Fargo reckoned they were going up a stream. Gabe kept telling him to duck low when they were coming to brush. Several times the blindfold was scraped off and he'd tell Matt to pull the bandanna up across his eyes.

They carried on sporadic talk, Gabe carrying the burden of conversation. Before long Fargo learned Gabe's last name was Monk. Gabriel Monk had started as a Ladderer ranch hand and worked up to foreman, until . . . Fargo wasn't quite sure. He got the sense of it, finally, when Gabe ribbed Matt about fainting at the graveyard.

Matt cried foul. "You'd crap your britches, Gabe Monk, if Azrael Tripp hoaxed you. Ponca ain't laughin'. I wonder if he knew how Jack got killed and Tripp killed him to keep him quiet?"

Jack Ladderer had died four months after the first renegade attack, Fargo learned. Jack and Azrael Tripp, Junior, had gone to buy cows, the valley's herds having been decimated during by Karnes' raids. But only Tripp returned, all shot up and leaking blood, leading a strange trail crew. They'd fought off a rustler horde, he claimed, and during the third day of pitched and running battles, Jack Ladderer was hit in the left eye and died instantly, the back of his skull blown out. They had to bury him on the range.

Tripp had hired the trailhands, claiming he was better prepared against attack. Some folks admired his push. Others disapproved of his shove, but soon learned that if they resisted, they'd get the worst of the deal. The men who took his orders were tough, hard, and liked to prove it.

Tripp now ruled Blockade Valley and ramrodded the Ladderer outfit. He'd cast aside the Karnes clan as useless to him, and fired any Ladderer loyalists like Gabe Monk. Nobody in Tripp's band of ruffians was from the Mormon families who'd followed Deacon Jophiel Ladderer into exile here. Tripp's gunfighters were renegades who had filtered into Blockade Valley. And if he had his way, Rachel Ladderer would be the Queen of Renegades—and of his harem of plural wives. No love, little lust, all politics. Tripp had seized power away from Deacon Ladderer, but a marriage of families would add legitimacy to his rule. And it would be quite a blow to his main opposition, the deacon.

"Rachel might just marry him," Matt said. "Azrael Tripp is a first-class lady's man. I've seen her look at him like a kitten lickin' cream."

All this and more Fargo overheard before they finally halted.

Dismounting, he was lead on foot by Gabe for a short distance, then allowed to pull the handkerchief off. He saw nothing but blackness. The air felt cool and clammy, and he knew he was inside a huge cave. Somewhere was the sound of running water.

Gabe struck a match, lit a lantern, and Fargo was able to make out the few spartan furnishings. A rock cooking hearth had been built where the draft would clear fire smoke, and Gabe began laying a fire in the hearth. There was a whiskey jug on a table next to the hearth, and getting the fire started required Gabe to take a few pulls on the jug.

Fargo tried a swallow when it was offered; he thought his eyeballs were going to boil out as the ball-o'-fire whiskey ignited a hole through his stomach. "Maybe I better tackle some food before I drink further," he wheezed. "A man dies happier on a full belly."

"We'll eat when the deacon and Rachel show up," Gabe said.

About the time the fire got going, Matt came in from tending the horses, and Gabe remarked, "I wonder if anything's happened to 'em. They should've been here."

"One of the horses that was here is gone, that mare Rachel likes, and no sign of the deacon's horse. I can't tell that anything's been bothered."

Fargo unbuckled the money belt and laid it on the table, grinning faintly. "I can't chase the deacon. Keep it handy, give it to him when you can."

"I just hope it won't be too late. May be too late already," Gabe told him. "This is tithe money, paid bit by bit by us in quarterly contributions to the Church over years, from long before we moved to Blockade Valley. Deacon Ladderer was treasurer and custodian of the tithe fund. Rachel wouldn't know, for the women of Blockade Valley don't handle big sums of money."

"Nary a lick of money sense," Matt added. "When she showed here the other day, she refused to say one dang thing about where she had been, why she had come back, why she took the belt, what she'd done with it—nothing, except she thought she could get the belt back. Then Father told her it was the tithe money, and she started wailing. It sure sounded like she thought she'd run off with Pa's money, and not the Church's. But she still won't explain. Obstinate as a striped-assed mule."

"She may be the wisest, Matt. We've got to keep quiet about her, the way Deacon Ladderer did when he reported the tithe fund missin'. He didn't mix in a word about your sister. We'd all go a long ways to help her, and the deacon will understand and forgive her whatever she's done. But in the eyes of Blockade Valley, she'd stand condemned of a sordid affair with an Outsider."

"Whoa up! Nothing sordid about, was nothing at all!" Fargo protested. "Didn't know her name till the last minute, when the guy who caught her spilled it. If I'd been white-headed, cross-eyed, and covered with warts, it wouldn't have made any difference to her. She was afraid of somebody, or somebodies, and I was just a handy way to escape."

"This man who caught her, what's he look like?"

"Never saw him there inside rifle range. But he's got a laugh that sounds like seeds rattling in a dried gourd, exactly like your Azrael Tripp."

"Tripp! He may be tryin' to bag all the birds. Ladderer is responsible for the tithe money, with or without her, and if the truth got out, Rachel would suffer. Mormon law can be strict. The both of them might be locked up in the local jail, or maybe even get hung. This is a helluva thing, Fargo. No wonder Azrael Tripp is got onto your trail."

"Jophiel Ladderer sent him, then?"

"I wish I could answer that question. The money was absent and so was Rachel, and despite the deacon's official story, Azrael Tripp is cunning enough to have put it together. He's wolfish enough to have gone to the deacon with a secret proposition to trail you, get back the money, and return it in secret—provided the deacon would marry his daughter to Tripp. But I doubt if Tripp would ever return that much money to Blockade Valley, not for Rachel or any other woman alive . . ." Gabe stood up. "We've got to get this belt back to Deacon Ladderer," he said abruptly. "I'll go in town, check there, Matt. You better go out around the hill circuit."

Nodding, Matt started to leave. Fargo glanced from him back to Gabe. "Guess I can't do any good out there," he said, "only harm. Just the same, you're taking a long chance, trusting me alone here, a rank stranger."

"Rank is right. If you're of a mind to, have a bath and wash your duds out while we're gone. You're welcome to what you can find here. We'll eat when we get back, whenever that be."

Gabe hastened outside, joining Matt and heading for a nearby lean-to where the horses were stabled. Fargo went along, retrieving his saddlebags and weapons, then returned to the cave. They accepted him now—or at least did not treat him as an enemy.

Fortified by a nip of whiskey, the Trailsman located the bath in a boarded-off cubby at the rear of the cave, fed by the water he'd heard—an underground stream pouring in through a crevice, splashing across the rubbly floor, and gurgling out through another hole. The cubby was like a roofless outhouse, plankboard-sided, with one skinny door; and the bath was an old horse trough dug in the streambed, the water flow keeping the tub brim-full and fresh. And cold.

Luckily Fargo brought the jug along with his soap, razor, and change of clothes. After a warm-up, he settled in the trough for a hard scrub. He had rinsed clean and was lifting the jug to ward off chills when a quick step sounded outside and someone tried the latch, then banged on the door.

Fargo put the jug aside and picked up his straight razor. "Who's that?"

"I thought so! Hiding in there won't help you!"

"Rachel!" Fargo breathed the name with a show of dismay. "I'm not hiding, I'm taking a bath."

"You can't fool me! Or scare me away by threatening my modesty! A girl doesn't live in a big household without seeing men in all states of undress. Now, open this door or I'll kick it in."

Fargo got out of the trough. Better to let her in, he figured, than invite trouble by trying to keep her out. And he was feeling just enough whiskey to not give a damn anyway.

10

Fargo shot the bolt back, half-forgetting the straight-razor gripped in his hand.

Rachel entered like a gust of wind. She saw him then, wet, stark-naked, looking at her partly indifferent, partly defiant. She flounced to a halt, frozen agape as he stepped nonchalantly back into the trough.

" 'Evenin', Rachel. You sure made yourself scarce."

"Fa-father didn't show up on schedule, so I rode out but didn't run into him . . ." She paused, then whirled and crashed the door shut. "Never mind me. Did Gabe or my brother bring you here?"

"Together, yes."

"There's not enough brains in the lot of you," she cried, "to form a pimple on a fly. Why did you follow me instead of doing what *I* told you to?"

"Well, a debt was overdue."

"What are you talking about?"

"I never thanked you for saving me."

"You moron!" Her eyes seemed to contradict her tongue, though, and after a breath she went on, less furious, "The man who waylaid us, named Tripp, runs Blockade Valley. He didn't make boss by being soft or stupid, and he's the best rider and hunter and shootist I know. He's got a hard-boiled crew backing him, watching the passes and patrolling the trails, and they'll cut you down for trespassing before you could say howdy. That's why I told you to keep rolling, to keep away and the belt safe."

"You're an odd one," Fargo remarked. "Most women I've met were either good or bad. You must be some of both, or you'd have quit this Tripp."

"I was never so close to slugging a man—and didn't."

"You swore to go with Tripp and abide by the Law," Fargo said. "Made for a long-term risk, and was one reason why I didn't wait to come after you."

"But I didn't swear to abide with Tripp," she countered, sitting down on the rolled rim of the trough, pouting winsomely. "I was hiding here till the boys eased off searching for me and I could slip out of the valley safely. I was going to find you, wherever you were, then bring the belt back before they'd spot me or get on my trail, with Tripp no wiser."

"That's another reason I didn't wait. I couldn't. The wagon train was already besieged by renegades knowing I had the belt."

Rachel trembled as if hit. "Honest, I didn't tell anyone."

"You didn't have to. A guy was seen with you, and it probably took just some simple tracking and asking around to get a line on me."

"If they tracked you, then, Skye, they might read your prints now and know you're here. Or Tripp may sense it, by instinct." She stroked her forefinger pensively along his shoulder and neck. "Dead-sure, they'd go manhuntin' you."

He eyed her, feeling stirrings, thinking she was in a manhunter mood, too. "They're not alone, Rachel. Olin Karnes brought in kith and kin."

"Ears everywhere. I was afraid Karnes would learn of the money."

"Well, Olin may lose interest after settling his account. Magee and Wayland are also mixed up in this somehow, I dunno what with and I dunno what for. Yet."

Her lips moved. "Magee and Wayland." That was all. She was leaning over him as her hand teased across his upper back and far shoulder, so close to Fargo that he could feel her warm breath against his skin. He was smart enough to sense she knew more and was trying to avoid being questioned; he was man enough to respond to her diversionary tactic. He stretched out afloat in the trough, and her eyes grew smoky and hungry as she gazed down at him.

He chuckled. "How's this for a third reason?"

Her pink tongue glided across her lips. "I was hoping to freshen up after my ride, so . . ." Tauntingly, she began stripping off her man's style workclothes, her firm breasts swaying gently as she tugged her panty-drawers down, exposing a frothing mass of red bush between the cheeks of her slender rump.

Fargo glanced hastily at the door. "Better hook the latch."

"What for?" Rachel asked, putting a foot in the water.

"Well, eh, your brother and Gabe might show up."

"Let 'em wait for their bath." She settled down facing Fargo.

"There's something to be said for this," Fargo remarked genially as she started to run a soapy washrag over his torso. "We'll be next to godliness while we're at it."

"Well, it's obvious to me now a Gentile isn't any better than a Mormon," she said, working the cloth along his thighs. "All you ever care about is poking a girl."

"What's wrong with that?" Fargo took the cloth and rubbed it up and down her legs and into her groin. "You like it, don't you?"

"Let's not discuss it," Rachel sighed, lounging with

124

her legs slightly bent and spread, while Fargo soaped and cleansed and stirred her to a feverish arousal. The brush of kneading hands across her breasts, the feathers of his fingers stroking her nether lips, his gentle kiss of her trembling lips, all combined to evoke in the girl an erotic stupor. She raised her face and pressed her open mouth tightly against his, her hand searching down between them. Fargo couldn't help gasping as the tease of her fingers closed around his throbbing erection.

"Not all guys are all the same," she murmured in a low, throaty voice as she rose and turned around to face his feet, his legs stretching between them. Placing his taunting shaft against the opening of her moist sheath, she prodded Fargo into herself with her trembling fingers, then squatted down, swallowing the whole of him up inside her quivering belly. Leaning back against him, she purred, "This *is* nice . . ."

Fargo thought it was pretty nice too. He could feel her body pulse as she undulated her buttocks against his pelvis, her thighs splaying to allow him greater access as she hooked her calves over the side of the trough. He rubbed her crevice, tweaked her clitoris, his other hand massaging her breasts, while she pumped smoothly upon his rod with a pressuring squeeze, matched rhythmically by strokes pistoning into her loins.

"Yesss, this is nice," she repeated shakily. "How'd you know?"

"Well, I've generally found it nice before."

"I mean, how'd you know seeing a naked guy makes me willing?"

"I don't know," Fargo said while thrusting upward. And he didn't. How can any man know anything about a woman? Not that he gave a damn about that or anything right then, except the exquisite pleasure building explosively within him. In any case, his vague answer seemed to satisfy Rachel, who moved more ardently as she also neared completion.

"If I'm getting too loose for you," she gasped above him, "I can put my legs together. That'll pinch me up tighter."

Too late. Fargo didn't even have time to tell her never mind as he climaxed violently up inside her. She shuddered, convulsing, crying out orgasmically. He collapsed limply, and she lay panting, pressing firmly back against him, exhausted, satiated . . .

After a long, lazy moment, Rachel climbed from the trough. "When you're dressed," she said as she toweled dry, "I'll draw you a map on a piece of scrap paper. You won't have any trouble following it."

"You mean—"

"I mean get out of Blockade Valley!"

"I'm not finished here," he said stubbornly.

"You're so finished," she snapped, wriggling on her shirt, "the undertaker would bury you as quick as a grave was dug!"

"I'm fine," Fargo said, regretfully watching her pull up her pants. "Just hungry. I kind of worked up an appetite."

Rachel started to move away, then stopped and swung around, her face a pale blur across the path of dimness that separated them. "Be a waste of good food," she retorted furiously. "You're a dead man here and just don't know it."

Then the door slammed and Fargo was alone.

Shortly, while in the trough scrubbing his muddy clothes, Fargo heard Gabe and the boy arrive. They were gratified to see Rachel, but it was clear that Deacon Jophiel Ladderer had not been located. The smell of sizzling food and boiling coffee began filling the cave, and driven by hunger, Fargo hastened out of the tub and into his clean clothes.

"Even a condemned man gets one decent meal,"

Rachel allowed when she served Fargo. It was good grub and plenty of it, and the coffee had whiskers on it. Afterwards, while his washed shirt and Levi's dried before the fire, Fargo cleaned and reloaded his firearms, and listened.

Talk was of a casual sort, a light diversion from the looming threats confronting them. Small mention was made of Azrael Tripp and his doings, and Rachel remained close-lipped about filching the tithe money. Mostly they were concerned about Deacon Ladderer, their worry deepening as the night lengthened. The fear grew that he'd been cut down by a drunken renegade, or ambushed by one under orders—though Rachel insisted Tripp knew better than to risk that. Besides, the deacon often played a lone hand and at times was gone for a day. He'd been late the last time he'd had a rendezvous with Rachel, slowed by the task of eluding the trackers he'd spotted behind him.

Deacon Ladderer had told his children how to reach this cave he had discovered, following his battle with the renegades in the pass. Rachel, Matt, and John had been elsewhere, and met him back at their Ladderer ranch. Back at the smoldering ruins of the log house, the funeral pyre of his three wives and their kids, who'd fought off the renegades till out of bullets and the renegades torched the house. The three surviving children had brought their father here and cared for him until he recovered from his wounds. Except for Gabe Monk, the cave had been kept secret against another such black day.

For all his searching and trailing, Azrael Tripp hadn't located it. He might have if he'd taken the blindfold trip, Fargo thought; with sharp senses and some diligence, the trail might be backtracked. Few had taken that trip, but to Fargo's surprise, the few included Magee and Wayland.

"They came only once," Rachel informed him, "and

that was when me and Gabe fetched them blindfolded, when Father had bought off that pair of curs. Father bribed them to escort the women and children out of the valley, to the nearest Mormon settlement. One went; the other was held hostage until Father got a letter from the settlement stating the refugees arrived safely. Wayland lost a coin toss and stayed. He was turned loose when Magee brought back the letter."

"They had to fight their way out because by then Azrael Tripp Junior had fetched in his renegades and taken the Ladderer ranch and all the rest of the valley," Gabe added. "Deacon Ladderer had killed old Azrael Tripp. Just before that, Porter Karnes finally got too rank for Tripp Senior's strong stomach, so they shot him down. But compared to Azrael Tripp Junior," Gabe declared, "Karnes, Magee, and Wayland are a trio of angels."

Fargo just happened to catch the quick sharp glance young Matt cut his sister Rachel. Her face flushed and she gave her brother a warning look.

And what he overheard after a few hours of shut-eye, when they took him out into the early morning to show him the lay of the land, clinched it.

Fargo was standing alone on a high point that overlooked much of the valley, focusing the pair of old army field glasses they had handed to him. He heard Rachel's voice. From the slight echo, she must have been standing in the cave mouth.

"If Azrael gave you a note to deliver to me, hand it over."

"Your father would take a gun and kill you if he ever found out about you and Tripp!" Matt's voice sounded brittle. "Your mother would turn over in her grave if she had a grave instead of burnt ashes. Your mother—"

"Was as good as your mother. Even if she was a Ute squaw. You give me that note Azrael sent!"

"I kept it in the pocket of that slicker Skye lent me, so if the rain's soaked the glue off the flap, don't claim I opened and read what that murdering lizard wrote his sweetie—"

There was the spatting sound of a hard slap. Matt's brittle laugh sounded like smashed glass. Fargo heard the rustling of his saddle packs, and a moment later he caught a glimpse of Rachel stamping out and off behind the horse corral with the still-damp note Tripp had given Matt to deliver. There was a red blotch on Matt's cheek when he joined Fargo, and his eyes were hard gray steel and his grin was thin-lipped.

"I'll kill that long-geared, spur-jingling son of a Tripp, to do the job my brother Jack left behind."

Fargo gripped the boy's slim shoulder. "Don't tackle it single-handed, friend."

The color that cold fury had drained away came back into the cheeks of young Matt. He managed a faint grin. Fargo went back to studying the valley with the field glasses . . . and gave a sharp grunt as the glasses picked up a lone rider coming up the valley but following no trail. Then the horseman was lost to sight in the brush that flanked the little river.

"Dammit, I got just a quick look and no more . . ."

"Maybe it's Azrael Tripp," Matt suggested, "calling to court."

"I wasn't thinking of Tripp." Fargo pointed. "Right about yonder's where I lost sight of him."

"That's where we come up along the river last night. That's the way you get here without leaving a horse track. Tripp don't know how to get here, nor does anyone in his outfit."

"It wasn't Azrael Tripp."

Half an hour passed. Fargo kept the field glasses trained until Gabe chanced to mosey over, then handed them to Gabe, saying, "All I got was a quick look and he was gone. But whoever he is, he knows how to get here and he's on his way. You don't suppose it could be Deacon Ladderer?"

Gabe shook his head. "No, siree. Not in broad daylight. He wouldn't risk being sighted and followed here to give away the cave." He made a motion for Fargo to follow him, and picked up his carbine. "If that's somebody we don't like, I'll show you how we stop 'em in their tracks. Fetch your gun."

With his Sharps in the crook of his arm, Fargo followed Gabe along a steep, twisting trail and out onto a flat rimrock that hung like a shelf over the trail. The trail was no more than a stone's throw below. Matt, who'd tagged after them, said one man could stand off an army here.

"Yonder's your rider, Skye. And it ain't Deacon Ladderer!"

It was Magee on a piebald mare.

"Stand your hand, Magee!" Fargo motioned Gabe back. He stood on the edge of the rimrock, Sharps pointed at the rider.

"Figured I'd locate you here, Fargo." Magee grinned up at him. "I was telling Wayland only yesterday while we was slippin' around Olin Karnes' camp, that the sign read like Karnes was pushing to overtake, and you was still on the long dodge. Which you wouldn't be if Karnes had cut you down and taken Deacon Ladderer's tithe money belt off'n your carcass. When we come to find you didn't throw in with Tripp's gang, me'n Wayland called a misdeal and shuffled 'em again. And we're in shape to deal you a pat hand."

"Maybe," Fargo said, keeping Magee covered, "I don't want no part of your game."

"Maybe." Magee sat hunched in his saddle like a jockey, his eyes bright and beady, paying no attention to Fargo's rifle. "But most maybe you'll want cards. You sure as hell ain't winnin' nothin' for nobody with this bobtail flush that's so weak it can't even try to bluff."

"And with you and Wayland in the game—"

"And with Magee and Wayland dealin' 'em like they got 'em marked, everyone here can't lose. Buck us, and everyone here will lose bad."

Gabe, stepping to the rim, growled, "It can't be more money you want, Magee. You and Wayland bled the deacon white. What do you want?"

"Why, I guess a Mormon blessin'," the little man replied. "Me'n Wayland is taking over Blockade Valley. We're willing to take the Ladderers out of this coyote hole and set 'em back on their home spread. There's room for us all."

"The deacon does the blessin's, but I can guess what he'd say. You would have him condone the crimes and sins of murderers. No!"

"Do you know where your prize deacon is?"

"Do you?"

"Sure do. He's hogtied in the big cabin used to be a meetin' house. Tripp's fixin' to fire-squad Ladderer tonight. Like you seen 'em do Ponca."

"And like I bet he done John in, too," Matt snapped.

"The boy's plumb right," Magee said. "It happened on our range, but me and Wayland had nothing to do with it. Ponca was ramrodding our MW at the time, and Tripp made some kind of dry-gulch deal with Ponca. Me'n Wayland never had a hand in it, that's no lie."

"The renegades who invaded Blockade Valley gathered at the MW. They rode from your ranch to here; Magee and Wayland, leeches, rode with them. Can you deny that?"

"We risked our necks to get them Mormon women and kids outta this valley, too," Magee said. "I'm not here on trial for past sins of Magee and Wayland; I come to make a deal. Me'n Wayland is getting along in years. All we want is the valley to run our cattle. And peace. Side me'n Wayland, we'll set Deacon

Ladderer free. It's your one and only chance. That's no lie. Now you playing what we deal you?"

Gabe glanced at the boy and then at Magee. "Yes."

Magee knew the trail to the hideaway; he'd been blindfolded, but he had figured it out to this point as he went along. Now he was going to go back down into the settlement, and Matt wanted to go with him immediately. But Magee said there was no rush because they had to wait till dark.

"Me'n Wayland gambled on your throwin' in with us. You couldn't do otherwise. So Wayland is doing his end of the job down yonder. We got only one man planted with Tripp's outfit, but he's a good'un. Or a wrong'un, accordin' for the way you size up a man that hires out for fightin' wages. Now, he'll slip a gun inside Ladderer's shirt and loosen the ropes on his hands while they're marching him to the cemetery. And when the jackpot's open, the deacon can take his own part. Wayland will be bushed up somewheres in short gun range. And there'll be me and you, and Fargo. And maybe young Matt, here. How many men has Tripp got?"

Matt said Tripp had a dozen renegades, maybe fifteen. Magee said he and Wayland figured about fifteen, and the odds didn't scare him. Magee and Wayland hadn't counted on Ponca getting killed, but they hadn't dared risk fetching more men. Too many cooks spoil the batter. Magee and Wayland had always bucked the big odds, he said, swinging his horse around to head back.

"We've had to travel together. There's times when me'n Wayland gits so sick of the ugly sight o' each other we're ready to kill us off. But we got to stick together. This is the furtherest we been separated in years. And it makes me uneasy. It might be our bad luck. Together me'n Wayland can lick big odds. Split us up and we might get cut down."

"We'll meet you tonight, at the cemetery," Gabe confirmed. "Till then, God protect you, Magee."

"Me'n Wayland," Magee said, "never took no stock in Gawdalmighty!"

When the piebald mare carried Magee down out of sight, Fargo, Gabe, and Matt hiked back to the cave. "I don't trust Magee and Wayland," Gabe said to Fargo, "but somehow I know Magee ain't lyin'. Tripp's going to stand Deacon Ladderer up and fire-squad him. We need Magee and Wayland."

"The same as Magee and Wayland need you. There will be time enough after the ruckus is over for them to deal with Ladderer." Fargo surveyed the hills piled up around the valley slopes. "Olin Karnes is playin' for big stakes, too. Good chance he's on one of those timbered pinnacles right now with his field glasses, and he could ruin it for us, Gabe, ruin everything."

"I don't follow."

"You heard Magee. Karnes is camping somewhere near, stalking me for the belt. If he tracks me to that old cabin where you were, that'll put him too close to here, too big a possible threat. He could foul up things tonight ten different ways from Sunday, but he'll probably side with Tripp, since I'd be on the other side. He has to be taken out, if at all possible."

"Yeah? Well, now? Stake you out as bait?"

Fargo pondered for a long moment, then said thoughtfully, "Not too bad an idea of yours, Gabe. Instead of a stake, I'll use the belt as bait. Remember how Magee automatically assumed I had the belt? A man like him would never believe I'd turn over that money to anyone. I bet Karnes is likewise. So spread around town that you found me. You swallowed every lie I told you, then left me some food and I went on my way, with the filled money belt."

Matt intervened, saying he ought to speak with Rachel about their father, but there was no sign of her.

Gabe suggested that like as not she had bushed up somewhere close enough to look and listen to what went on between them and Magee, and was still on her way back. Matt went out to look for her, and Gabe and Fargo took the moment to make some changes in the belt's contents. It's closed pouches were full of wads of scrap paper, cloth, anything handy that made it bulge convincingly. Gabe tied Deacon Ladderer's tithe money up in a canvas bag and hid it away.

"I hope this lure will fetch Karnes my way," Fargo said, buckling on the belt.

"Won't be easy, Skye. Olin's like his pappy Porter, a coiled rattler, only he cut off his rattles and strikes without givin' warning. Since early childhood he's been trained in dirty work. There isn't any bushwhacking tricks he doesn't know." Gabe held out a huge hand. "Good hunting, friend."

Fargo clasped the hand and grinned flatly, nodding.

Matt came into the cave. Tears dimmed his eyes and there was a grim set to his jaw. Rachel was not with him. She was gone. Her horse was gone. Rachel was on her way down into the Blockade Valley.

11

The game was on.

If Olin Karnes was an expert in this game, then Skye Fargo could play with equal cunning. But as Fargo had learned long ago, for all his sharp wits and acute senses, the best way to outwolf the likes of Olin Karnes was to let Karnes outfox himself. Considering Karnes was hunting the Trailsman in the middle of unfriendly country, Fargo bet Karnes would be playing it cautious right now, taking his time.

It led Fargo to suspect that Karnes might haunt that ramshackle cabin near the point where Fargo's tracks vanished. Karnes would be suspicious and on guard against any of Tripp's renegades coming around, for whatever reason. And he would be wary and watchful for the chance that Fargo might return back down the river. So Fargo played the hunch that Karnes would not stay too far from the cabin in the clearing. That was why he was working his way back there.

Like any scout worth his salt, Fargo had a trained faculty for remembering a strange range. During that early-morning stint with the binoculars, he had gone over the terrain as far as the lenses could reach. And as near as a man could map its topography without traveling it, he knew it and had it mapped in his memory so he could travel it confidently. It was a winding, twisting course he reined the Ovaro along, halting every now and then to strain his eyes and ears, then riding on. Circling back, stopping, waiting, then moving off in another direction—it took patience, and he approached the vicinity of the cabin with the skulking caution of an Indian.

The tumbledown shack looked forlorn in daylight, deserted, and somehow sinister. Fargo had hidden the horse in the brush and come on foot the last quarter-mile or more, and now he crouched behind the tall, thick brush and gripped his Sharps and waited. He watched the cabin, and also the brush beyond it where scraggly willows and underbrush grew among the boulders.

Suddenly Fargo tensed. Then he heard it—the snorting sound of a horse. Seconds later he heard it again, closer, as well the noise of cautious movements in the brush and scrub juniper.

Simultaneously a man's voice called, "Olin? Olin?"

Olin did not answer. Fargo heard the brush crackling as though somebody were easing stealthily, perhaps apprehensively through it. But the man had discarded all caution with his mouth, spewing out lurid profanity.

Then, startling, from a point in the heavy brush rose a gravelly voice, "What's chawin' at your guts, Floyd?"

A string of vile oaths came in reply. "Damn your skulkin', Olin! If you expect me to feed you, get out here where I can see your hide!"

"Quit bellyaching and get a fire started while I slip the pack. An' scout around yonder side of the willows for a place to stake the horses."

"Do this, do that . . . Christ! I ain't your servant, I'm your brother—"

"Half-brother. And the devil knows how many more such half-brothers I got like you. Porter Karnes had more damned wives than Solomon. Only reason that pa of mine throwed in with the Mormons was so he could marry all the gals." The chuckle was rasping and ugly.

"That's a damn lie! You made it up to build yourself a tough rep, Olin. Pappy Karnes was a good Mormon!"

"So good they had to kill him off," Karnes jeered from the brush. "Porter Karnes was a liquor-swilling, woman-lusting butcher. I ought to know, I'm his oldest son, and he taught me what I know until Old Tripp or Ladderer blew his eyes out. Now, get that fire started and quit sniveling, or I maybe get to thinking you're more bothersome than useful. You know what, then, Floyd? Maybe I'll split your skull and slit your guts and let the wild boars root on you."

Fargo waited until the cheery blaze of a cook fire glowed through the willows, and he caught a brief glimpse of a man moving toward it in the brush. And he guessed it was Olin Karnes. Then he moved cautiously around the clearing to a place where he could hide and watch.

The man called Floyd was twenty, give or take a year. He was gangling, with big hands and feet, dirty brown hair, and a face only a buck-toothed weasel could love. He looked crafty and treacherous, capable of slitting the throat of a sleeping parson.

The other was Olin Karnes, of course, but Fargo reckoned he'd have recognized the man from descriptions given by the Talbots. He wore a buckskin shirt with most of the fringe worn off by hard usage, and his buckskin pants were tight around the saddle-muscled thighs. He was of average height, but his body was larger and heavier than average. His nose was lopsided, one ear was cauliflowered, and his eyes and course hair were the brown of chocolate that had lain around too long.

Karnes stayed back in the shadows while Floyd cooked their meal. Fargo squatted watching, thinking it couldn't stay that way forever, and silently moved into position with his Sharps. He waited at ease, ready to snap him . . .

At last Floyd told Karnes in a sullen whine to come and get it. Only then did Karnes move out of the shadow into the clearing. Fargo waited patiently for the moment he knew would come. The two men settled in and began to eat, swilling coffee that smelled like it would strip paint.

Suddenly Karnes dropped his plate. Drawing his revolver while springing aside, he swiveled around while intensely staring at the brush. Fargo shifted and brought up his Sharps, irritated yet impressed by that intangible sixth sense that had seemingly warned Karnes of imminent danger. It was hard to develop, yet it could mean the split-second difference between life and death . . . and Karnes was very much alive as he crouched there, with his long-barreled pistol thumbed to full cock, his eyes squinting around.

"Lay it down, Olin," the flat-toned voice of Azrael Tripp yelled from the bushes, "or I'll collect my own bounty on your stinkin' hide!"

Fargo lowered his Sharps, realizing that he had better not shoot till he learned how Tripp was involved and how that changed the odds.

"That you, Tripp?" Karnes bared his big yellow teeth. "Then keep your shirt on. Me and you oughta have a medicine talk."

"I could gut-shoot you, Olin, then beat all I need to know out of Floyd's hide."

"Hell, you don't think I'd trust this sneaky pup with anything important, do you?" Chuckling, Karnes holstered his revolver. "But he can shore make chow, and this is the first warm meal I've had since the day before yesterday. Floyd, you can tell Tripp what you know . . . For a teaser."

"Rachel Ladderer," Floyd whined, "is gone."

Tripp snorted. "She's hiding from me, I know all that."

"No, run off," Karnes said. "Gone from the valley."

Behind his brush shelter, Fargo gripped his Sharps, straining to hear.

"Where'd she go?" Tripp snapped. "Spill it out, Olin!"

"That, Tripp, is what you'll have to pay me to find out."

Tripp cursed Karnes in his vicious, flat-toned voice. Karnes paid no heed, picking up his tin plate and loading on more food to replace what had dumped onto the ground. Floyd shifted about uneasily.

Tripp quit his foul cursing, and there was an uneasy silence. Karnes cleaned his plate, drank his coffee, then picked his teeth with the point of his hunting knife while Floyd began cleaning up the dirty utensils.

Tripp broke the silence, finally. "What makes you think I got money?"

"You taken that scout's trail."

"What'd that pay me?"

"Quit trying to play poker, Tripp. That wagon scout got away with all the Jack Mormon tithe money in Blockade Valley. Tell Tripp how come we know about it, Floyd."

"I was outside Gabe Monk's window," Floyd said, licking his weather-cracked lips, "when Rachel told him the deacon said she'd taken the tithe money. She bust out bawling. She said she'd clean up her own mess. Said she'd track the belt down and bring the tithe money back, but said she'd have to hide away a few days till she could leave. And it was then I seen you slip off from near where I was hid, Tripp. I pulled back soon after, before she let him hug her more and kiss her."

"You sneakin' whelp!" Tripp's voice was a flat-toned snarl.

"Don't murder me!" Floyd's whine built to a shrill scream.

Azrael Tripp's saddle carbine spat fire, and Floyd's

scream choked off into a terrible death rattle. He went down clawing with big, clumsy hands at his belly, his mouth open and his eyes wide with horror as death glazed them, and he pitched over into the campfire.

"Floyd was as sorry a cub as Porter ever sired. I don't know why he was so scared of kicking the can, but he was always scared of something." Karnes had not moved a muscle, although there was a stench of burning cloth and human skin rising pungently. Fargo felt a cold wave of nausea from the odor, the smell of callous barbarity, and heard Karnes continue in his rasping voice, "That's why Floyd always coyoted around in the dark, always seeing and hearing too much. Kept Floyd spooked all the time. Hell of a way to live. But you shouldn't have been so quick-triggered. Floyd hadn't told the whole of it."

"Drag your brother's carcass out of the fire," Tripp ordered. "He's commencin' to stink. Then take up where he left off."

Karnes got slowly to his feet. "Near as I recall, Floyd heard what he just told you while coyotin' and told it to me." Reaching, Karnes grabbed the dead Floyd by both legs and dragged the limp body clear of the campfire. "It was interesting but not needed. We were onto this scout, this Skye Fargo, thanks to your guys and them crazy Gideonites carryin' on 'round Fort Bridger. We knew he had something worth taking, but weren't sure what till Floyd told us. Yep, and Tripp, he wasn't done talkin' yet."

"And you talk too much, without sayin' anything," snapped the voice from the bushes. "Get on with it. What happened to Rachel Ladderer?"

"Floyd was comin' to that. She just up and run for it, Tripp. Floyd saw her ride out of the valley, and trailed her. You should've let him stay alive till he told where he followed her. A man your age should have learned by now to keep a lid on his temper."

As he talked, Karnes had reached out for the dirty canvas used to cover the kyacks that held the food, shaking it out as though to use the canvas as a shroud for Floyd. Then it happened—so suddenly it was done before Fargo could anticipate the move. And the same must have held true for Azrael Tripp. One second the canvas was flapping wide like a bedsheet on a clothesline; the next it was flung wide and upright like a curtaining screen. Hidden for that instant, Karnes dived headlong for cover. Tripp's carbine spewed jets of flame and the roaring echoes of its heavy explosions rocked the empty clearing. And then there was Olin Karnes' voice again, jeering, filled with venomous hatred.

"Let that learn you, Tripp! That whining Floyd would surely have spilled it all for you if you hadn't shot him—providing I didn't sling my blade into his mouth to cut his tongue off. Now it'll cost you that tithe money!"

Olin Karnes' rasping chuckle made a sound like a cackling hyena. And he stank like one. He crouched in the brush so near Skye Fargo that the Trailsman could smell the stench of his sweat and grease-glazed buckskins.

Fargo heard Tripp swearing futilely as he reloaded, cursing himself for letting Karnes outsmart him. Tripp might not be scared, Fargo reckoned, but he was probably badly rattled.

Tripp quit cursing, and there was a tense silence momentarily. Then he laughed—that deadly, flat-toned laugh Fargo had heard before. "What makes you think I'd be packing that tithe money on me?"

" 'Cause," Karnes said, "if you ever got your claws on that much *dinero*, you'd never let go of it. You got the deacon's belt strapped around you now, right next to your hide."

Tripp's flat laugh sounded again. "I'd give a lot to

watch you rip the clothes off my dead carcass and find no belt. I ain't got it, ain't seen it—not recent leastwise—and seen only a night glimpse of this Fargo."

"Fargo must've come here to throw in with you. No other reason to."

"He didn't. Guess the sign wasn't right." And again Tripp's flat-toned laugh taunted Karnes.

But it was short-lived. Karnes' chuckle blotted it out. "By hell, you must be slippin', you outthought yourself. I'll kill you and then pick up the wagon scout's trail."

"Don't make the mistake I made when I smoked Floyd."

"Meanin'?"

"Meanin' that two guns is better than one. We can team up."

"Don't make me howl, Tripp. I hate your guts."

"I'd rather be partners with a mad buzzard! But this Skye Fargo is a curly wolf, and hard to shave. You ain't exactly hung his pelt on the fence. And he must be a fast talker to've slid through Gabe Monk's hands with the deacon's tithe money. But he's still bottled somewheres in the valley, *my* valley. How far you think you could get before my men get you? Do we deal?"

"It's a deal."

The flat-toned laugh and the hidden chuckle mingled—an unholy duet. Yet neither of the killers would venture from behind the brush; theirs was a bond of hatred and treachery, and neither dared trust the other fully.

"What about Rachel Ladderer?" Tripp asked.

"I'll sell her to you at my own price later—when you got the tithe cash. Money still talks big, and till then, Rachel stays hid where you can't locate— What in hell's that?"

Fargo had thrown a rock.

He'd listened to them long enough, now. They might have stayed there all week, their guns ready to fire, still swapping taunts, each hoping and waiting for a killer's shot at the other. He would have gladly let them kill each other . . . But where was Rachel? Somehow he had to motivate them to go after her instead of him, so he couldn't pull any sort of spectacular stunt. A gunshot would get their attention—to see how fast they could run a mile. It was then he had noticed the stony chunk and felt how comfortably it fit his palm, how true it winged when he pitched at the cook fire. In that split instant before the rock smacked into the coffeepot and skillet, he had thumbed back the hammer of his revolver.

Now he banked on its startling, clattering effect. "All right, you men," he yelled, "That buys you my chips in this game."

Karnes exclaimed, "Well, I'll bone-damned!"

"You must be the wagon scout." The ugly chuckle was in Tripp's voice.

"That's right."

"You got that tithe money on you?"

"There's a money belt with the Ladderer brand on it buckled right around my belly. And it sure as hell isn't empty."

"The boy with all the marbles, Tripp." Karnes chuckled. "Might as well take him to a cleanin' here and now."

"You want this money," Fargo retorted, caustic, "but you're scared to come out into the open to fight for it. So I'm going to smoke you both out—winner take all." He unbuckled the belt with its bulging pouches, adding, "I've had all the damned hounding a man can stand. Here she comes!" Swinging the belt over his head, he threw it straight at the cook fire and it landed stretched out across the blaze. "There, you two craven-bellied coyotes, fight for it out in the open, or let it burn."

He heard Azrael Tripp's choked cry of horror, heard Karnes curse thickly, and he knew that both were now staring in shocked dismay.

Skye Fargo was backing away now, slowly, cautiously. He made hardly a sound as he slipped away from the trees and underbrush to where he had left his Ovaro. When he was at a safe distance, he quickened his pace and he was running with long strides over the last hundred yards. He was dripping with sweat and breathing hard by the time he reached the pinto. Mounting, he rode to where he had a long-range view of the cook fire, then reined up.

The voices of Karnes and Tripp carried, taunting him to come out into the open. When they got no reply, their uneasiness mounted. They knew this could be another trick to get them into the open. Or it could have been on the level.

"Get it, Olin, before it burns!" Tripp's flat-toned voice had a sharp, shrill edge to it now. "Yank it out of the fire!"

"Age before beauty, Tripp! You've got first dibs on that Mormon cash."

"Hey, Fargo, it's your game. Make your play!"

"That sidewinder ain't here, Tripp!" Karnes yelled. "I'm right where he's been bushed up. He's run off."

Dry brush rustled and crackled with action. Fargo couldn't tell which man made the first move, for both tore from the brush at the same instant. Tripp had the longer stride, but Karnes was fleeter of foot and a master of the boardinghouse grab, snatching the belt just as Tripp was reaching for it.

Stung, Tripp dived headlong at Karnes, wrapping his thick muscled arms around the buckskin thighs. They crashed in a tangle of legs and arms, landing on the dead Floyd, then rolling over and over, locked in wrestlers' grips. To Fargo, it looked like a hand-to-hand battle to the death. He gave a lean, sardonic grin at the irony of these two sharks murdering each other over a belt stuffed with worthless scraps.

Karnes still held the belt in his free left hand, his legs wrapped around Tripp, his hunting knife glinting in the firelight. But Tripp's revolver was clubbing down with vicious chopping blows at Karnes' skull. Karnes fought with desperate bull strength. The pistol smashed down with savage ferocity, and Karnes went limp. The knife was still clutched in his hand, but his eyes were closed, and blood clotted in his long brown hair.

Scrambling to his booted feet, Tripp took the money belt and a pistol off Karnes, then backed away, training his revolver. "Come alive, Karnes. I got the money, and now I want Ladderer's high-chinned daughter."

Karnes stirred sluggishly, getting to his hands and knees.

"You flash that toad-stabber at me," Tripp warned, "I'll gut-shoot you."

Karnes showed no interest, no fight as he stood slowly on rubbery legs. But this wasn't the end of it, Fargo reckoned. Karnes, as long as he lived, would loathe Azrael Tripp. And if Tripp should give Karnes any part of a fighting chance, there'd be another battle. Fargo was just gratified that Karnes was still alive, so he could pilot them to Rachel.

Tripp was taking no chances, keeping his eye and his revolver on Karnes. Then, using his free hand, he opened one of the pouches of the money belt. An angry snarl burst from his flat-lipped mouth. "That cheatin' bastard!" Enraged, he began hurling the scrap paper and cloth into the fire, cursing.

"You gone loco?" Karnes demanded, astonished. Burning both hands in a frantic effort to salvage the money from the flames, he took a better look, then abruptly stepped back. "We been had!"

"When you get done bull-roarin'," Tripp rasped,

"you can start taking me to where you got Rachel Ladderer."

"What about the wagon scout? You lettin' Fargo off that easy?"

"I'll kill that son of a bitch, if I have to cold-trail him into hell," Tripp snarled. "Get on your horse, Karnes."

"I'd like a shot at that Fargo myself. Stake me to my guns, Tripp."

"Screw your guns! I'd throw 'em away afore I'd give 'em back."

"Then I'll get along with this six-shooter I taken off Brother Floyd's carcass." The pistol showed suddenly in Karnes' hand, aimed straight at Tripp's belly. "Lay my guns on the ground. Me and you better quit fightin' and talk business, mister. Let's leave each other alone till Fargo's dead."

"All right, we'll bury the hatchet. Work with me and let me have Rachel, Karnes, and you can dance at my weddin' tonight. Till then, I need you to guard off that Fargo, and you need me . . ."

They led Fargo a twisting, winding, difficult trail to follow. Tripp and Karnes were artists at being able to blot out a warm trail so thoroughly that a tracker would lose hours picking up the sign again. So Fargo followed close on their tracks. But not too close.

If it had been tough going before, then it was doubly dangerous now. For though the chase was reversed and Skye Fargo was now doing the trailing, those two would suspect he might be trailing them and would be ready for anything. And when he sighted rough country that looked as if it might be a good place for an ambush, he approached it warily or rode wide around it.

Toward dusk, Fargo caught glimpses of the scoundrels through the trees and boulders, as they rode to a brushy patch of rough country. Within ten minutes, he saw the wispy smoke of their early cook fire and approached in a roundabout detour, covering his tracks. He could not put it into words or explain to himself why, but when the smoke ceased ten minutes later, he got a strange feeling that maybe he was nearing the end of the trail. And he thought perhaps that strange sixth sense was warning him that Tripp and Karnes planned to slip back and murder him.

Fargo was moving cautiously across the broken country in the direction of the place where he had last seen the smoke of the cook fire. But he traveled in a looping half-circle, so that he approached the place from the far side. He rode up on the camp before he realized he was so close, abruptly sighting a saddle horse and a mule grazing at the end of long picket ropes. But there was only one horse. Either Tripp or Karnes was in the saddle and on the prowl. And the thick underbrush hid the man who remained in camp.

Then the picketed horse nickered and Fargo crammed his hat like a nosebag over the muzzle of the Ovaro. Somewhere in the growth a few hundred yards away, another horse nickered in reply.

Standing at the pinto's head, his Sharps gripped in his hand, and well-hidden in the brush, Fargo watched. He was rewarded by the brief glimpse of Azrael Tripp delving through the foliage about a hundred yards away. The picketed horse and mule lowered their heads in a few minutes and went back to their grazing. Fargo heard and saw the cautious movements of Tripp become more restless and nervous, and it was a long time before anything happened.

Olin Karnes rode out of the dusk, his cayuse traveling at a long trot. Close behind followed Rachel, her wrists tied to the saddle horn, the reins of her moleskin grulla snugged to Karnes' saddle ahead. Blistering the air blue with curses, Karnes brought both horses to a halt and sat astride his blowing cayuse looking pleased.

"Told you I'd bring her. There she is, Tripp, no harm done."

"Rachel?" Tripp called from the brush. "You hurt at all?"

She shook her head. "I'm okay."

" 'Course she is!" Karnes swung off his weary horse, heading for Rachel. "Squaw camps ain't my favorite hangout, but squaw mothers are good women. They treat guests right and mind their business. Honester than whites, too, never even poached the liquor . . ." He tilted a big jug, drinking, then went with his knife and cut Rachel loose. "C'mon out, Tripp, tell the lady hello and share a drink!"

"It's taken you a long time to get back, Karnes . . . And it's half an hour anyhow since your horse nickered out yonder."

"Our horses never nickered. We ain't slowed from a high trot since we left the camp. Say that again, Tripp! What horse nickered?"

"Mine. There on the picket rope. And a horse out yonder, the direction you just came. I'd swear there's someone bushed up in the other direction. Drink hearty, Karnes, an' drink alone. I ain't making a target out of myself."

Karnes went back to his cayuse, yanked off his saddle and bridle, and turned the horse loose. Then he threw the saddle on the bare back of Tripp's picketed horse and jerked the picket-rope knot free from the horsehair rope fastened to the rawhide hackamore.

Tripp growled, "What's he doin', Rachel?"

"Leaving you afoot," she replied.

"Does look like he aims to," Tripp agreed, his flat-toned laugh sounding from the brush. "Karnes, I'm gonna change your mind with a bullet, you stinkin' gut-eater! I been waitin' too long already."

Tripp's carbine cracked and the bullet whined so close to the ears of the horse that it spooked, rearing. It almost jerked Karnes down when the weight of the pitching horse hit the end of the hackamore rope. He had to let go or get dragged around until he could swing the bucking horse to a halt. So he let the horsehair rope burn through his hand, and for once in his cunning bushwhacker life stood in the open to fight for his life, his gun ready.

"No use tryin' to coyote, Karnes! I'll drop you for a runnin' target," Tripp called, stepping out from behind the scrub junipers. "An' now I'm killin' you, Olin Karnes." As he spoke, the saddle carbine in his hands began spitting streaks of flame. The carbine held by Karnes spewed answer.

The two fools gave no thought for Rachel, caught in their sudden fury. She didn't swoon or panic—her grulla did. It bucked and winged, sunfished, pinwheeled, and flung an especially berserk four-legged fling, all in the midst of the gunplay, and all Rachel could do was hang on for the ride.

Fargo had been crouching beside his Ovaro. But at the crack of the first shot he was in the saddle, spurs raking, bent low along the neck of his charging horse. He crashed through the brush as bullets whined and snarled like hornets past his head. He rode toward the crouching Olin Karnes and kicked both legs from the stirrups, quitting the saddle with a jump that landed him not a dozen feet from where Karnes stood on thick-bowed legs, an empty smoking carbine gripped in his hands. Karnes dropped the carbine and clawed for his revolver. And in those split seconds, Fargo got in the first shot—a gut-shot that doubled up Karnes and swayed his burly body on widespread legs.

Tripp drew his revolver, then, and opened fire on Fargo.

Fargo back-pedaled, pivoting aside, almost ramming into Karnes.

Then one of those twists occurred that make life interesting.

From the nearby shadows of brush and trees emerged three men. At a run they were coming with guns drawn, and in that first instant, Fargo thought they were Tripp's men. Tripp turned on them like the enemy, though, and then Fargo saw their faces, saw how they had a certain family resemblance to Olin Karnes. Karnes must've been set to double-cross Tripp all along; he'd had only to lure Tripp into view, and his hidden death squad would do the rest . . . and they might do it yet.

The men were coming fast. Tripp had disappeared faster, nowhere to be seen, and Rachel was regaining control of her horse. Olin Karnes was an arm's length away, chuckling as he took his time dying. Fargo leapt at Karnes, knocking him down and tearing his pistol away. He whirled to confront the three men, who were now perhaps thirty feet away and fanned right, left, and center.

One of them laughed heartily. It was like a signal for them to make their move, and there followed a crash of guns that sent horses snorting and lunging at their ties.

Fargo twisted in a corkscrew crouch, triggering behind and before, Karnses' gun in his left hand kicking with recoil, the Colt in his right seeming to discharge of its own accord.

The man in the center was the first to be hit, a slug punching through the top of his skull and killing him instantly. He did not so much as twitch when he fell. His right arm remained extended, his fingers wrapped around his revolver.

The man on Fargo's right was struck next, in the middle of a loping stride. He cried out and threw up his arms, face contorting, and then another bullet ripped upward through his pectorals and emerged from the nape of his neck. He dropped sideways with both hands pressed tight around his throat until his life had run out.

The man on Fargo's left stood his ground firing; the fusillade seared about Fargo, nipping his clothes, spraying dirt, whining by his face and body. The lead from Fargo's Colt shattered the bone in the ambusher's thigh, but the gunman was still firing as he started dragging himself back to cover. He began raising himself slowly, triggering desperately, the slugs from his wavering carbine coming amazingly close, burning a groove in the knee of Fargo's pants. An answering bullet drilled him in his heart, and the man collapsed without sound.

Fargo rose cautiously, looking around . . .

The flat crack of a hidden derringer sent him diving. A stinging arrow nipped his earlobe, and with a croakish laugh, Olin Karnes moved on for a second shot. And then Fargo was blasting at Karnes' face, the face that must have haunted Elaine and Julia Talbot in their nightmare dreams. He could not miss. His slugs tore into the forehead between the slitted eyes to drill a black hole there and blast out the skull with its grungy brown hair. Olin Karnes, the late head of the Karnes clan, was dead on his feet before his thick bowed legs buckled and he went down with a heavy crash into the brush.

Fargo stood for a moment, breathing heavily, then walked over to where Rachel was calming her horse. He looked up at her with a tease of a grin and said, "Think of this trouble, next time you want to run away."

"I wasn't running away," she retorted coolly. "I was flat-out snatched." The girl sat ramrod-straight, frowning, her glance flicking from Fargo to her rowdy horse and back again. Suddenly she snapped out at him, "Don't look at me! Turn around, quick!"

"That's too old a trick to fool a man."

Her eyes blazed at him. As suddenly as she'd spoken, Rachel now leaned forward in the saddle, neck-reined the grulla a quarter turn, and raked her spurs. The grulla lunged tight-angled at Fargo an instant before the blasting report of a handgun.

Fargo, hastily wheeling to avoid the horse, saw that he had indeed been a blind fool. Azrael Tripp stood between the pillared trunks of two trees. In his fist was a Dancer .44 revolver, still smoking, still held leveled at where Fargo had stood with his back to him.

The grulla had suffered the slug marked for the Trailsman, the bullet slicing into its flank. Twisting in midstride, the screaming horse thrashed frenziedly and one hoof kicked Fargo hard. There was an abrupt, blinding explosion inside his brain as he was knocked asprawl . . . and dimly, vaguely, he had the impression of Rachel going to Tripp, going with Tripp . . . But it was confused with the brilliant white light flashing behind his eyes, then winking into total darkness . . .

And he felt himself falling into a black, bottomless pit.

12

The stars were out and a round white moon rode the sky.

Skye Fargo and Magee sat on their horses behind the brush where the wagon bridge crossed the little river near the graveyard. Similarly hidden on the other side of the road were Gabe Monk and young Matt Ladderer. The three of them had met Magee here, just as Gabe had promised Magee earlier they would, and had split up to gain what little advantage they could against the expected great odds. Magee was uneasy, though. He dismounted and handed Fargo his reins, saying he was going to scout around afoot till he located Wayland.

"The son of a bitch was supposed to meet me here at the bridge. It ain't like Wayland to let a man down."

That left Fargo alone in an ugly frame of mind. He couldn't trust Magee. This could all be a trap the little weasel had led him into. But he'd had to put some kind of trust in the man. And Magee's uneasiness wasn't faked. For only the second time in years, Magee had kept repeating, he and his partner were separated. That took something vital out of Magee's fighting spirit.

The thought of Deacon Ladderer being held prisoner by a ruthless killer like Tripp was troubling unto itself. Despite Magee's assurance that Ladderer would be given a fighting chance for his life, Fargo was pestered by the fear that Magee was lying, or that the wily Tripp had caught onto Magee's man in his troop and killed the spy. That would mean Deacon Ladderer could have already faced a firing squad.

Fargo tried not to let Rachel Ladderer into his thoughts. But she haunted him like a ghost—a wanton spirit vanishing with the enemy. His body throbbed with pain, and his head pulsed to a savage ache as he again reviewed what had happened. There had been Rachel on her spooked grulla. When he had scorned her warning, she had ridden into him. A gunshot came from behind, then Fargo had a glimpse of Azrael Tripp with a smoking revolver, the horse lurching . . . He recalled being kicked by a flailing hoof, and after that there was nothing to recall until he came to, alone, Rachel long gone with Tripp. He'd been left no choice but to return here, to follow through with Magee's reckless plan against Tripp and, unfortunately, Tripp's willful, intended bride.

"Rachel read that letter Tripp sent her," Matt had asserted bitterly. "I hate to believe it, but she went to join up with that sage rat, and that's when Olin must've grabbed her. Wish they'd kept her. I'd rather see her dead than hitched to Tripp."

The waiting was the worst. Beyond the graveyard a half-mile away, the sounds of celebration could be heard: men letting out cowboy yells and shooting off guns, the scrape of a fiddle, now and then the high shrill squeal of a honky-tonk girl. There was a dance going on and the sounds of revelry drifted out across the weathered grave markers of the cemetery, a dance celebrating the upcoming wedding. Fargo could picture Rachel Ladderer high-stepping in the embrace of Azrael Tripp.

Then the fiddle stopped, the shouting faded away, and there was a silence more ominous than the shouting. Out of the silence came the thudding of shod hooves, and men on horseback rode into sight.

Azrael Tripp rode in the lead. In the middle of the column of heavily armed riders rode one man whose hands were tied behind his back. The prisoner weaved in his saddle, slouching forward as though he were drunk. He was bareheaded and his hair and whiskers were matted with dried blood, and his shirt and undershirt had been ripped to shreds.

Behind Fargo sounded a choked curse. It came from Magee, back from his scouting trip. "It's Wayland! The devil in hell!" He jerked his bridle reins from Fargo's hand and swung up in his saddle without touching a stirrup, his revolver gripped in his hand. "They got Wayland!"

"Take it easy, Magee." The low-voiced warning came from the shadows behind. "Don't go off half-cocked."

A man rode out from behind the heavy brush. A short, heavy-shouldered man with untrimmed iron-gray hair and beard, he peered from under craggy brows with a pair of eyes that held a strange look. They seemed to look at Magee and on through him and far beyond. Alongside him rode Rachel Ladderer, saying not a word, her expression hidden by darkness, cradling her saddle carbine in the crook of her arm.

Magee gasped. "The deacon!"

"If I ain't," Deacon Ladderer replied, white teeth showing through bearded lips, "then I should be jailed for impersonating."

"Tripp had you prisoner." Magee's face was gray. "Now he's got my partner Wayland."

"There was a swap made," Deacon Ladderer said. "Rachel here handled the deal. She told Tripp she'd take him and his tough hands to where Wayland was bushed up, but he'd have to turn me loose and let Skye Fargo leave Blockade Valley alive. If Tripp kept his end of the deal, she'd marry him and I'd do the ceremony. Tripp took her up on it mighty quick. They caught Wayland napping. He put up a whale of a fight, but they ganged up on him, and when they fetched him back to the saloon, Tripp turned me loose to go fetch my Book." The deacon held up his leather-bound Book of Mormon, adding, "Hadn't gone a mile till Rachel overtook me, told me you would be some-wheres near the graveyard. She'd overheard you, Magee, planning things with Gabe and my son Matt and this Fargo fellow."

Magee was staring gimlet-eyed at the men on horse-back as they came riding up to the cemetery. There was cold murder stamped on his face, and he had his carbine levered, ready to fire. His eyes drilled the man who helped Wayland down off his horse.

Tripp was riding back and forth like he was on fancy parade. He had a bottle in his hand and kept taking nips at it as he gave his ramrod order. "Stand that fool Wayland alongside his grave," he called out. "You six firin'-squad men take your places. Get your minds off whiskey and women long enough to hold a bead. I gotta get back and slick up. A man's gotta shine pretty at his own wedding."

Deacon Ladderer bared his teeth, his eyes slivers of cold steel. "I was hoping, Magee, you'd want to stop that wedding."

The four saw Wayland walking slowly toward the open grave and lidless pine-board coffin. A man walked along behind him with one hand on the prisoner's bound wrists, while Tripp lined up his firing squad. They were all dismounted now, all partly drunk, Tripp waving a bottle and cracking obscene jokes about his wedding night to the roars of his crew. Then it happened.

Magee gave a shrill whistle. The sound of it turned the heads of the firing squad, and the other renegades whirled around to stare at the heavy brush near the wagon bridge.

Wayland no longer had his wrists tied. His arms

swung free, a revolver clutched in each hand. And the man beside him gripped a saddle carbine. They jumped in behind the saddled horses ground-tied nearby. Their guns roared, their first salvo hitting three of the firing squad in their backs. Then all hell tore loose.

Magee spurred out from behind the brush, firing as he went. He was cursing his partner Wayland in a harsh, shrill voice with all the names he could lay tongue to. Wayland and the other man—obviously the spy they had planted in the Tripp crew—vaulted into an empty saddle and charged out at Magee bellowing profanity. It looked for a second like they were going to shoot each other out of the saddle. They reined their horses just in split-second time to avoid a pileup and they both yelled as their stirrups locked and they charged, their guns spewing death, at the dozen renegades on foot.

"Fight, you renegade sons," Wayland bellowed.

"Let's hit 'em," Gabe shouted from across the road. Instantly he and Matt, and Fargo from his side, launched into action, plunging toward the fray like an avenging tidal wave.

With yells of shock and pain, Tripp's vicious renegades dived behind grave markers or tried to escape out into the brush. Fargo and the others charged into the scattered ranks, shooting and yelling, their onslaught turning the cemetery into an inferno of pounding hooves, rearing horses, and blasting guns. Repeatedly the renegades were repulsed, thrown back or shot down, yet repeatedly they rallied in frenzied efforts to burst out of this death trap, firing a deadly response.

Magee and Wayland's rep was killed almost at once, but for a time it looked like Magee and Wayland themselves led charmed lives, their tough hides bulletproof. Then suddenly their horses were shot from under them, and they stood back to back, cutting down the remaining odds against them. Both partners were bullet-riddled and dying on their feet, but too tough to die until all the renegades had been maimed or killed off. There was something splendid about that last stand of those two miserable coyotes. Grim and heroic. They begged no quarter and gave none.

The muzzle of a renegade gun was shoved from behind a grave marker at Fargo. A gun bellowed a little to the Trailsman's right and a bullet from Gabe's dragoon plowed along the exposed arm and passed through the man's neck. Simultaneously, Fargo threw a shot at Tripp, but it was a miss and the bullet hit one of the men standing close by.

Tripp reached out and pulled this man against him as a shield, just as Fargo felt the cold rush of another slug. Turning, Fargo answered with two shots, spotting the renegade behind another grave marker, which saved the man from having his head torn off. But the burst of splinters ripped his face wickedly and the partly deflected slugs tore away half of a high-boned cheek.

The renegades who'd clotted around Tripp had either fled or, save for four or five, were all dead. Tripp was left standing alone, a powerful arm clutching that dead man against him. Now he took the sagging weight on his left arm while his right hand leveled his revolver, seeking targets. Rachel stood near the bushes at Tripp's left, and Fargo thought, though he could not be sure, that some word the girl had uttered had reached the ear of the renegade leader.

Fargo sensed Tripp's terrible fury and the direction it would take, and he set himself in motion. Tripp's revolver cut a fast arc in the direction of the girl, and Fargo checked his rush, realizing abruptly that he could not reach Tripp before Tripp caught Rachel under his sights. He set himself for a shot that must both avoid the dead man and hit Tripp above the shoulder line.

But Tripp, turning back toward Fargo, was offered a stationary target.

It was Azrael Tripp who was overanxious now. He fired before his gun had completed its full swing, and knew the game was done. Fargo drove a bullet home into Tripp's gut. Tripp faltered, the dead man slumping from his nerveless grasp, pain twisting his face as he struggled to pull his gunhammer back.

Fargo triggered and snapped down on an exploded shell, his Colt empty. He saw the revolver in Tripp's two hands, its barrel lifting. The man was dying, yet he could still aim a gun with both hands and pull the trigger. Fargo heard Tripp's taunting laugh . . .

Then a pistol blazed behind Fargo. The revolver in Tripp's hand spat flame and its bullet plowed into the dirt in front of the Trailsman. Tripp, shot through the head, lay dead. And Fargo saw young Matt Ladderer with smoke drifting from the muzzle of his pistol and a grin on his pallid face.

"I got him!" Matt's voice sounded thin and shrill. "He killed my brother Jack and I killed him." The gun slid from his hand, then, and he began to retch.

Nearby, Gabe stood with his gun in hand, like some grim executioner. Magee and Wayland were both dead, but most of Tripp's renegades had been sent to hell ahead of them.

Rachel came hurrying across, ordering her brother to go wash his face, he was a disgrace puking like that.

Matt grinned sheepishly and said to Fargo, "Don't let my shrew of a sister ever get something on you. You remember that, it'll come in handy . . ."

Fargo said he'd remember. After Matt left to go clean himself, Fargo commented to Rachel, "That's not all I'm remembering. You took the money belt, but for more reason than just to run off. Otherwise you wouldn't have gone to all the trouble of sneaking a ride across the Green. And back when you saved me, you said you'd been in the storeroom of the Mormon post, and let me believe it was because you were filching supplies. But that's not why. You went to bribe Magee and Wayland, like your father had once before. You hoped to hire them and their cowhands to fight Tripp, wasn't that it?"

"I was desperate. I couldn't think of any other possible way to save Blockade Valley," Rachel admitted, nodding. "I never loved Tripp, I couldn't, but I never hated him. Not until he wrote me that last note. If I hadn't agreed to marry him, he would've killed you as well as my father, and he swore he would've come after me and kill anybody else who tried to stop him. Satisfied, Outsider?"

"Satisfied, Mormon."

When they had dug a trench big enough to hold the dead renegades, and a double grave for Wayland and Magee, and had Azrael Tripp's grave dug, it was daybreak. Silhouetted by crimson dawn, Deacon Jophiel Ladderer recited from memory at the graves of the dead, for the middle was missing from his book of Mormon, a deep cut-out for the .25 single-shot pistol nestled hidden within. And when those graves were filled, he stood there, a smile on his bearded face. His daughter had given Tripp her promise to marry him, and the deacon had fetched along his Book to perform the wedding ceremony. And a gun to kill the bridegroom.

13

A banjo was strumming when Fargo got back to the Kentucky wagon train.

Sunny skies and the last few days of rest, these were salve for nerves drawn to the snapping point, and the settlers were in a singing mood, deploring earlier grumbling. Smooth sailing ahead. Wishful thinkers were beginning to brag that they'd soon cross the Sierra Nevada and look down into flowering California. And they all would have gladly tarried awhile longer, if Fargo would have allowed them the luxury.

"We're rolling on," he told them. "We're late, thanks to mud and the fat I worked off your bones. When time warrants a breather, I'll order it. Another month, maybe."

They took his pessimism as a crusty joke, laughing despite disappointment. A month? They winked at one another. They'd be settled on rich California lands before that, as any half-wit could plainly see.

Fargo smiled to himself. He'd bring them across the Sierra, all right. He'd halt them at Lookout Point for that look at swimming California distances. But first he'd lead them across wastes of sage and lava hills, with remote and forbidding sawtooth mountains. First he'd take them through hell.

LOOKING FORWARD!
**The following is the opening
section from the next novel in the exciting
Trailsman series from Signet:**

*THE TRAILSMAN #72
CALICO KILL*

*1860, the Oklahoma Territory
just above the Kiamichi River, where
respectability and savagery hid behind
the same mask. . . .*

They were a lynching party. He'd seen enough of them to know at once. Only there was a difference. Not in type or attitude, those were usual enough. Six of them rode raw-faced and calloused, men who enjoyed lynching, taking coarse glee in the anticipation. Their victim rode in the center, and that was typical. Wrists tied behind the back. That was the same, too. But there the usual abruptly ended. No burly cowhand sat in tight-lipped defeat. No rangy horse thief rode with head bowed in guilty resignation. This victim was a slender figure in a dark-green blouse and skirt to match, high breasts bouncing in unison with her mount's stride, her medium-brown hair swept up and back from her forehead and held atop her head with a turtleshell clip.

Fargo moved through the thick stand of horse chestnut until he was almost parallel to the riders. He'd just wakened and breakfasted in the cool shade of the forest when he heard the horses nearing at a gallop. He had the Colt in hand as they appeared beyond the foliage along an open stretch of ground, and he had frowned at once. He never liked lynching parties, most self-serving and all aimed at shortcutting the law. Hanging was one thing, lynching another.

He'd swung onto the Ovaro and sent the magnificent black-and-white horse through the trees as he followed the riders, and now he reined to a halt as they came to a stop. The girl was young, with a pert, pugnacious face, a small upturned nose, and round cheeks, he took note. If she was afraid, she didn't show it. Anger and defiance held her face and he saw medium-brown eyes flash at the men that surrounded her.

"This'll do," the front rider said, and indicated a buckeye with a long, low branch made for a lynch rope. He dismounted, a thin-faced man with thin lips, reached up, and pulled the girl from the saddle.

"Bastards," she snapped as she hit the ground.

"We ain't gonna let all that go to waste, are we, Hawks?" one of the others said out of thick lips and a puffy face.

"Meanin' what?" The man called Hawks frowned.

"We might as well enjoy her first," the other one said. "The boss ain't gonna care any."

"Guess not," Hawks said, and the others left their saddles to gather around the girl. "Me first, though," Hawks agreed.

"Bastards," she hissed. "I didn't do it, damn you."

"You were seen, by more than enough folks," another man chimed in.

"Dooley saw you," the beefy-faced man said.

"He does nothing but lie and cheat in that card palace of his. He'd do the same anywhere," she snapped.

"Polly saw you," Hawks snarled.

"It wasn't me she saw," the girl shouted.

"And Cyril Dandrige saw you hightailing it down the road. Everybody knows that dark-red cape you wear," Hawks added.

"It was stolen a few days ago. I never knew it was missing," she said. She held to her story, Fargo observed. But then she'd have to do that much, he realized.

"Cut the damn talk and let's get a piece of her lyin' little ass," one of the others interrupted.

The thin-faced man closed his hand around the neck of the girl's blouse. "You better enjoy this, bitch, because it's going to be your last screw in this world." He laughed harshly.

"Go to hell," the girl flung back.

"Untie her wrists so's we can get her clothes off. I like my piece soft and naked when I get it," the man with the beefy face chortled.

"Just tear them off, dammit," another shouted impatiently.

Fargo's eyes swept the six men as they crowded around. His eyes took in the way each of them moved, the hang of their arms and the cut of their bodies, and he glanced at their hands and the six-guns on their gun belts.

"Wait," he heard the girl say, and returned his eyes to her. "I guess there's nothing else but to enjoy it if it's going to be my last time," she said.

"Count on it, tramp," Hawks growled.

"Then untie my hands and I'll make you enjoy it more," she said, and Fargo felt the frown press itself across his brow and he peered at the girl. She suddenly seemed resigned, an instant change in her that surprised him.

"Untie her," Hawks barked, and one of the others

used a knife to slit the ropes holding her wrists. The girl brought her hands in front of her as she rubbed circulation back into her wrists. Slowly, she began to unbutton the blouse as Hawks waited in front of her, his eyes widening with anticipation. The others backed a few paces as they shifted their feet in coarse glee.

"This'll go quicker if you help," she said to Hawks, and the man stepped close to her and began to undo the lower buttons.

Fargo stared at the girl and felt the surprise still pushing at him when she suddenly exploded into action, her hand snapping out with the quickness of a young cat to close around the six-gun in the man's holster. She yanked it out in one lightning motion, but she had to take precious split seconds to turn the gun in her hand and Hawks had the chance to fling himself away from her. But the shot caught him high on the shoulder and he let out a cry of pain as he fell back.

Two of the nearest rushed at her as she whirled and brought the six-gun around to fire again. She got off another shot that grazed the temple of the beefy-faced one. "I'll take at least one of you with me, you rotten bastards," she screamed, fired again but with too much haste as the third man ducked, came in low, and tackled her around the knees. She went down as she fired a harmlessly wild shot before the others closed in on her. She fought with the fury of a wildcat cornered as they grabbed at her and Fargo saw her legs kicking out, her hands trying to rake their faces with her nails. But they took hold of her, finally, Fargo saw as they yanked her to her feet. One of them smashed his hand across her face but drew only a curse from her.

"String her goddamn neck up," Hawks shouted, and Fargo saw him pressing a kerchief to his shoulder.

"Just kill her." The others obeyed and began to drag the girl to the tree where one quickly looped the rope across the low, thick branch.

Fargo sent the Ovaro into a fast trot while he was still in the trees and emerged into the open less than a dozen yards from the men. He saw them hold on to the girl as they turned in surprise to stare at him.

"Party's over, gents," he said almost affably.

"Who the hell are you?" Hawks snapped.

"Delegate from the antilynching society," Fargo said. "Just let the girl go and we'll all stay friendly."

"The hell we will, mister. Get your ass out of here or we'll make it a double." Hawks pressed the kerchief harder against his shoulder.

"That so?" Fargo smiled, his hand resting on the butt of the big Colt at his hip. "I think I'll turn that down. So will the young lady. Now just let her go."

"She's a goddamn murdering bitch," one of the others shouted.

"The law call her that, yet?" Fargo inquired.

"We don't need to wait for the law. We know, and lynchin's too good for her," Hawks snarled.

"They just want to lynch somebody," the girl snapped.

"She killed the finest man in town," one of the others said, a big, burly man with small eyes, avoiding the girl's accusation.

"We'll let the law decide that," Fargo said.

"I'll tell you one more time, mister. You ride fast or you're a dead man," Hawks rasped.

"Hang 'em both," one of the others put in.

"Can't ride off," Fargo said calmly.

"Why the hell not?" Hawks bit out.

"Against my principles. Got a prejudice against lynchings."

The one with the beefy face stared at the big man on the Ovaro. "You must be loco, mister. There are six of us," he said.

"Damn," Fargo swore. "My mama always told me to learn to count." He saw them exchange quick glances suddenly filled with uncertainty about this big, handsome man who faced them with unruffled calm. Fargo smiled inwardly. That would make their moves even more nervous and unsteady, and he surveyed the group again. Hawks was already no threat with his injured shoulder. The two men to his right, Fargo had already noted, were slow-moving and cumbersome. Their gun hands wouldn't be any faster. That left three standing alongside one another, two that might be of average quickness, and the third, the burly figure, had thick-fingered, heavy hands more able to wield a smithy's tongs than a six-gun.

Fargo waited and watched the uncertain glances harden. Like most men with more surface conceit than real courage, they had to prove themselves in front of one another, and he expected that, too. As the two on his left started to draw their guns, he had the big Colt out of its holster and in his hand with one smooth, lightning-fast motion. The two shots sounded almost as one and the two men collapsed in a heap against each other, one with blood spreading from his chest, the other with his abdomen gushing.

Fargo swung the Colt as the two slow-moving figures at his right had just cleared their holsters. He fired again and the two figures went down as though pole-axed. Fargo brought the Colt around and saw the thick-fingered man drop back, fear on his face as he kept his hand away from his holster. Hawks started to move for his gun, winced, and thought better of the idea.

"Drop your gun belts, nice and slow," Fargo said, and the two men carefully complied. "Get on your horse, honey," Fargo said to the girl, and watched her pull herself onto the mount with a flash of sturdy, well-turned calf. "Walk your horse next to me," he told her.

He turned as she came alongside and began to walk the Ovaro very slowly, but his wild-creature hearing was tuned to the two figures he'd left standing behind him. He caught the faint sound the moment it came and cursed inwardly, the soft slurred sound of leather suddenly creasing, the sliding hiss of a gun being pulled from its holster. Fargo whirled in the saddle, the Colt steadied against his abdomen. It was the burly thick-fingered man, crouched on the ground with the gun just drawn out of the gun belt he'd dropped. Fargo fired as the man raised his six-gun and the burly figure catapulted backward, straightened out in midair, and dropped flat onto its back. The man lay still except for a last gurgling sound that sent tiny bubbles of red from his lips.

"Damn fool," Fargo murmured, and his gaze bored into Hawks. The man pulled back and slumped to one knee, only abject fear in his face.

"I won't try anything, honest, mister," he pleaded.

"Ride," Fargo said to the girl, and sent the Ovaro into a trot. He rode back into the horse chestnuts, following a deer path through the forest until he finally emerged onto a cleared slope where a stream bubbled its way downhill. He halted, swung to the ground, and watched the girl pull up and dismount. As the horses made for the stream, he took her in more carefully and saw medium-brown eyes blink at him out of her perfectly pretty face. But a tiny furrow touched her brow beneath the upswept hair and she regarded him with a mixture of gratefulness, curiosity, and a dollop of wariness.

"Why'd you do it?" she asked, "I'm grateful to you. Good God, I am. But why? You could've got yourself killed."

"Didn't expect that to happen." Fargo smiled and watched her regard him with her brown eyes narrowed.

"Guess not, seeing the way you handled that Colt," she said. "But why? You could've gone your way. Most would have."

Fargo shrugged. "Don't like lynch parties. Never have," he said.

"Then I'm grateful for that, too," she said. "Saying thank you doesn't sound near enough for having saved my neck, but I've no other words for it."

"They'll do," Fargo said. "You've a name?"

"Clover," she answered. "Clover Corrigan." Her eyes waited.

"Fargo . . . Skye Fargo. Some call me the Trailsman," he answered. "Now you want to tell me your side of this, Clover Corrigan?"

She half-turned away for a moment and stared into space. She had a neat, solid figure, bustline very high and very round, a sturdy shape with curves in the right place but everything put together compactly. "I can't tell you much of anything," she said.

"Who was it they said you killed, the one they called the finest man in town?"

"Douglas Tremayne," she said.

"You knew him well?" Fargo asked, his eyes peering sharply at her.

"I worked for him," she said. "But I didn't kill him."

"Sounds like he was found dead and you were seen hightailing it," Fargo said.

"It wasn't me," she snapped angrily as he searched her face for the slightest sign of hesitation or slyness. But the only thing he saw flash in her pert face was anger and indignation.

"What about that dark-red cape they said you wore?" Fargo pressed.

"I didn't even know it was missing. Somebody took it to set me up."

"Why?"

"I don't know, dammit," she said, and Fargo saw the frown dig harder into her smooth brow as she stared back. "You don't believe me, do you?" she said accusingly, with a touch of hurt in her voice. She was either very clever or very innocent, he decided.

"I didn't say I didn't believe you," he answered.

"You as much as said it. Do you or don't you?" she insisted.

"Can't say," he answered honestly, and saw the instant anger flare in her brown eyes.

"Then you're the same as they were," she snapped.

"I'm not trying to lynch you," Fargo said quietly. She took in his answer with a glower. "You're asking me to just up and believe you. You've no right to ask that."

'   "Why not? I didn't do it."

"I've been fooled by words before. Pretty faces, too. Believing takes more."

"I haven't got more, not now," she said. "If I'd time, maybe I could find out more. I have to."

Fargo let his lips purse. She had an angry directness that held no guile in it. But, he reminded himself again, some women were mighty fine actresses. "You saying I should just let you go your way," he remarked.

"Yes, so's I can find the truth of it," she said.

"Or head for Texas," Fargo said, and she flared at once.

"You're making it awful hard to stay grateful," she threw at him.

"Let's ride and I'll listen some more. There's got to be more you can tell me, maybe more than you know there is," he said.

She shrugged as the glower remained, and climbed onto her horse with a quick, angry motion that made her high, round breasts bounce.

Fargo began to lead a slow pace along the slope and kept his questions calmly casual. "I passed through Two Forks Corners a day ago. I take it this all happened back there," he said.

"Just outside of town, at Douglas Tremayne's house."

"Tell me about him."

"He was the town banker, leading citizen, popular with everybody. He was handsome, smooth, about forty but looked thirty."

"What'd Clover Corrigan do for him?" Fargo questioned.

"He hired me about a year ago. I helped him with whatever he needed, from making coffee, filling in as clerk at the bank, seeing to his appointments, to cleaning up his house. Sometimes he'd keep me late into the night writing down thoughts he had for a speech he was to make. Sometimes I'd fix dinner for him. I was part assistant, part maid."

"Anything else?" Fargo asked.

"No, nothing else," she snapped angrily. "I know that a lot of people thought that, but it wasn't true. Douglas Tremayne and I were never really close. For all the things he had me do for him, none of it was ever anything real important. I never did really know him. I always felt that."

Fargo watched the troubled frown wreath her pertly pretty face. For all her anger and glower she had a lostness to her that reached out. She rode alongside him completely unaware that he had made a wide circle back toward Two Forks Corners. "Who were those men that wanted to string you up?" he asked.

"Hawks is a two-bit horse trader that Douglas Tremayne lent money when no one else would. Ahern, the big one, was the town smith and drunk. Douglas kept him in business, too, just as he did with the others. Hell, the whole town would've been with them by afternoon. Douglas Tremayne was everybody's friend. He sure wasn't the average banker," Clover said.

"Where'd they get to you?" Fargo asked.

"Came to my place. I'd just finished dressing when they dragged me out. I'd been home all night, but they wouldn't believe it and I couldn't prove it," she said.

"Not with all the folks that saw you running," Fargo commented.

"Not me, dammit. They didn't see me," Clover exploded.

"You any ideas who they saw?" he asked, and watched her closely as she frowned in thought.

"No, not yet," she said slowly. "In that cape of mine, it could've been anybody, even a man."

"I suppose so," Fargo thought aloud. "Tremayne have a girlfriend?"

"I can't say for sure, but I suspected he did. Once I found a blue slipper with a red bow in his closet, like someone forgot to pack it away before leaving in a hurry. As I said, for all I did for him, there was a lot about him I never got to know."

Fargo pulled up as they finished the full circle and let the Ovaro graze on a patch of sweet clover. Two Forks Corners lay north, just beyond a thick stand of cottonwoods. All the time they'd talked he'd watched her and had seen no sign of glibness or guile. But he saw her watching him, picking up the thoughts that moved across his mind. "You've done a lot of asking and you're thinking all you've got is more words," she said.

"That's right." He smiled wryly.

"Because I can't give you more yet," she flared. "I've got to find out what happened myself."

"How do you figure to do that with a whole town waiting to lynch you?" Fargo questioned.

"I don't know." She frowned. "I'll find a way. There's got to be a way, someplace to start." She halted and turned a long glance at him. "You could help me."

"I already did that," he said.

"I know, and that sort of makes me your responsibility," Clover tossed back with a smugness coming across her face.

"What?"

"Well, it does. Hawks is going to tell about you, and that Ovaro's easy to spot," she said. "They'll say I killed Douglas Tremayne and you helped me escape. You've got to help me."

"Damn, you've more than your share of brass," Fargo growled, and she shrugged and was suddenly quite happy with herself. But she did have hold of a kernel of fact and he didn't want more trouble. "I stopped a lynching. Nothing wrong in that," he said. "But I'll tell you what I'll do. I'm in these parts to break trail for a cattle drive down into Houston. I'm a week early. I'll help you, but we'll do it my way."

She smiled, a sudden explosion of sunniness that turned her pert prettiness into warm loveliness. "I'll settle for that," she said. Something, perhaps a fleeting expression in his lake-blue eyes, caught at her and she suddenly turned a suspicious glance at him. "What's your way?" she asked.

"First, I turn you over to the sheriff in Two Forks," he said.

"Hell, you will," she exploded. "Oh, no."

"For your own protection," Fargo said.

"So you can get off the hook by turning me in and going your way," she shouted. "Forget it. You're out for yourself, just like everybody else."

"Being grateful has a short life with you, doesn't it?" Fargo said.

"Yes, when it comes to being put in jail," she snapped.

Fargo glared at her. "Damn, you're a regular little cactus," he said. "But I'm into this and I'm going to help you in spite of your suspicious, short-tempered hide. I'm taking you in."

She sat alongside him; her eyes searched his face and he saw them suddenly soften. "Maybe I am too suspicious. Maybe I should be thankful to you," she said quietly, and then, her voice tightening, "but I'm not," she hissed as she smashed both hands against him.

He felt himself go sideways off the Ovaro at the unexpected force of the blow, tried to stop his fall, but his hand missed the saddle horn and he landed hard on the back of his neck. He felt the sharp pain as his head hit a rock and the world turned gray, then black, and he lay still in the sudden slumber of unconsciousness.

He hadn't any precise idea how long he lay'd lain

174

there before he stirred, feeling the dull pain at the back of his head, and pulled his eyes open. He shook away fuzziness and the world took shape, the Ovaro, first, standing nearby. Fargo pushed himself to his feet, his hand automatically going to the holster.

"Damn," he swore as he found only empty leather, and he peered at the horse. She'd taken the big Sharps from the saddle holster, too, he saw and swore again under his breath. He pulled himself onto the Ovaro, let the last cobwebs clear from his mind, and saw the tracks where she'd turned and raced up the slope.

He started following the hoofprints and knew he wasn't at all certain whether he was following a scared, angry, brassy little package of fiery innocence or a very clever and determined pert-faced killer.